SEPTIMUS AND THE STONE OF OFFERING

SEPTIMUS
AND THE
STONE OF
OFFERING

STEPHEN CHANCE

THE BODLEY HEAD
LONDON SYDNEY
TORONTO

For Norman and May Owen,
who have taught me
to love Cymru

© Stephen Chance 1976
ISBN O 370 11033 1
Printed in Great Britain for
The Bodley Head Ltd
9 Bow Street, London, WC2E 7AL
by Redwood Burn Limited
Trowbridge & Esher
Set in 'Monotype' Baskerville
by Gloucester Typesetting Co. Ltd
First published 1976
Reprinted 1979

CONTENTS

I

Fire by Moonlight

Perhaps it was the stump where Sandy's left leg ended just below the knee that prevented the intended murder. Or perhaps it was the extra glass of whisky which caused the stump to itch and so woke him in the middle of the night. Otherwise the scandal would have echoed through the valleys of North Wales, and the tiny hamlet of Hafod Maenen become the centre of a newspaper sensation. As it turned out one man died and one nearly died, but otherwise only three people really knew the truth of what happened, and one of them remembered only very indistinctly.

Colonel Sanderson, D.S.O. and bar, M.C. lay in his bed and grunted. He rolled over restlessly and scowled up at the dark shape of his artificial leg hanging in its beckets. His hand slid down his thigh to scratch the stump, although scratching would only make matters worse. He needed the lotion in the bathroom cupboard, and that was a complicated journey, a crutch and forty feet away. Still, he reflected, heaving himself up, it was his own fault. Too much alcohol in the bloodstream always made the stump itch, and he had had more than a quarter of a century to get used to the fact. He rolled out of bed, groping for the crutch. The illuminated dial of the alarm clock proclaimed that it was a quarter-past three, a God-forsaken hour to be awake, but serve him right! He had been deep in Samuel Smiles' *Lives of the Engineers* before a sweet-scented log fire in the Mill sitting-room. Even engrossed in

George Stephenson as an example of 'self-help' he had known in his heart what the extra whisky would do. He adjusted the crutch under his armpit, and with the expertise of long practice thumped off to the bathroom.

He switched on the light and settled himself on the edge of the bath. The effect of the lotion was almost instantaneous, sharp and cold, as if he had dipped the stump into an ice bucket. He sat a moment, enjoying the sensation, then he hopped on to his one foot and threw open the bathroom window, leaning across the sill so that he could gaze out into the April night. It was still and silent except for the clatter of the millstream as it came down the hill and echoed hollowly, like its own ghost, in the channel beneath the window. The shadow of the wheel bulked large in the moonlight. Once it had driven slate saws. Now it drove the diverse machinery in Sandy's commodious workshop and provided amusement for the summer visitors. To his right lay the lake, Llyn-y-Moch, calm under an almost full moon, its surface shimmering like shot silk. Beyond the lake the mountains were sharp against the night: Cnicht, stark as an alpine peak, Moelwyn Bach like a trilby hat, the towering bulk of Moelwyn Mawr, the moon hanging over them like an incandescent balloon. Sandy looked down to the end of the lake. There was a mist rising from the water. It was like smoke in the moonlight, and in its middle there was a red glow. Sandy stared a moment before he remembered. It must be the brazier of the watchman on the site where the Electricity people were taking soundings to decide whether it was possible to dam the lake and turn the valley into a reservoir.

Sandy turned his mind away from an unpleasant subject. There was little enough he could do, even though – despite his engineering past – he wished the Electricity Board all the ill in the world. He had no wish to see the valley flooded, to have to accept compensation and seek a new home at his age. And he had more than a little sympathy with the marauders – Welsh Nationalists or whatever – who had broken into the site hut and thrown the equipment into the lake, and so made the watchmen necessary.

His eye travelled back along the blackness of the mountainside beneath the jagged line of the high peaks. Odd! There was another light, a bright pin-point just above the lake shore, clearly a fire. He frowned, trying to place it. Over there the mountains fell almost sheer to the lake in a precipitous line of cliffs, Craig-y-Moch, beloved of rock climbers. The fire was to the left of the cliffs, where the road which ran round the head of the lake petered out in the disused Craig-y-Moch slate quarry. He called to mind the details of the derelict workings: the abrupt incline, the piles of shattered rock and slate rubbish held back by crazy walls of unmortared slate, the rusting pipes, the ruined machinery, the dark tunnels leading into the labyrinth of the riddled mountains. At the bottom of the incline a few buildings huddled on the flat foreshore. There was a roofless barracks where quarrymen had once lived, the gaunt remains of the manager's house, its sad garden overgrown with unkempt rhododendrons. And there was the Maenofferen chapel – the chapel of the Stone of Offering. It also was a ruin, but a granite ruin, far older than the quarry. It belonged to a Wales lost in the mists of time, a Wales before Reformation and Revival had put their hands on Cymru, before even the English invaders had come over the marches out of the east bringing with them their own brand of Catholic Christianity to sweep away what had belonged to the Celt, what had come from Ireland and Iona, and before that from the forests and groves of the Druids.

Sandy closed the window and went back to bed. But he could not sleep. The fire had been among the quarry buildings, but who had lighted it? Rock climbers? Certainly they came this early in the year, and certainly they camped among the ruins. But not usually on a weekday, and anyway they had to come through the village. Usually they stopped to buy supplies at the village shop, the splendidly named Royal Stores. May Parry, who, with her husband,

9

kept the shop, and who came daily to the Mill to cook and clean, would surely have mentioned it. In that tight-knit community no stranger could pass without everyone knowing. And again, climbers certainly lighted fires, but not usually at three o'clock in the morning. The fire had obviously been close to the chapel – the chapel of the Stone of Offering. He suddenly thought of sacrifices, of legends of magic and mystery, of Druid groves and offerings to the old gods. Wales after all was the land of Celtic twilight. There were stories about the chapel, but he could not remember the details. They had not registered on his practical engineer's memory.

He was surprised by his own concern. A fire in the mountains? Odd, but why should it bother him? He realized that all the inhabitants of the valley were a bit on edge because of the threat that hung over their homes. Still puzzling, he fell asleep.

He awoke to fitful sunshine streaming through the window and the shrill voice of a woman raised in anger. It was May Parry, and she sounded very cross. In the Mill, with an instinctive courtesy which Sandy admired, she always spoke English, only lapsing into her natural Welsh in moments of stress. Sandy propped himself on one elbow, listening. For all the years he had lived in the valley, his unmusical North country brain had mastered only a few words of Welsh. He caught the word 'Pandy' which was the name of his Welsh collie, and the phrase '*yr hen ddiawl gi yna*', something about 'a devil of a dog'. He rolled out of bed, strapped on his leg, donned a dressing-gown and went downstairs. In the kitchen May was leaning over the bottom half of the stable-type back door hurling Welsh abuse into the morning. Gwyn, her five-year-old adopted son, was sitting on the floor, his back propped against the sink unit, half a trout clutched in his fat fist.

'Da,' he said, seeing Sandy and proffering the bloody remains of the fish.

'Morning, Gwyn,' said Sandy, and then more loudly, 'Morning, May.'

She turned, framed by the doorway, a dumpy little woman, spherical and comfortable. Her round face was pink with anger, her round spectacles seemed to sparkle like a short-circuiting dough-mixer.

'Colonel, that thieving dog of yours, that Pandy, *yr hen gena*. Stole the trout, he did. And Gwillym bought the brace from John Wesley Jones who caught them in the llyn yesterday with our Gwyn for company, as he always does, bless him. Both of them for your breakfast, and they a pound and a half on the shop scales. You should drown that Pandy, Colonel, really you should, and me setting to fry the two of them . . .'

Sandy set about stemming the flood of her Celtic ire.

'Never mind, May. I'll have the one that Pandy left.' He picked up the child, removed the remains of the trout and hastily substituted the kitchen timer, so cutting off the lusty wail of protest gathering in the infant lungs. He twisted the timer so that it started to tick, held it to Gwyn's ear and sat down on the kitchen table, the child in his arms.

May busied herself at the cooker, mollified as she always was by the Colonel's surprising expertise with the little boy. He was a good man, and a pity he had never married. But the War, she supposed, and that old leg of his . . .

'May. Were there any visitors through the village yesterday? Climbers or some such?'

She slit open the belly of the trout with the macabre ease of long practice.

'Climbers? Not that I heard. There was an engineer man from the dam electrics. Wanting to buy Panatellas, he was. Gwillym said he said – the dam electrics man – that they were going to grind Cnicht to powder to make their dam. But that was only talk. But no. No strangers. Why do you ask, Colonel?'

'Nothing,' he said. 'It's not important.'

After breakfast he got out his battered Land-Rover and drove the hundred yards to the Royal Stores. As he clambered out

Pandy came down the road from the Mill. His hindquarters were wagging violently from side to side. The dog was intent on re-establishing friendly relations after his essay in crime. Sandy patted his head. 'Pandy old son, you're a rogue and a villain, and you look just like a member of the Mafia having an audience with the Pope.' He ordered the dog into the Land-Rover. 'Stay there. Stay. I forgive you, though I doubt if May will.' The dog yawned and curled up on the passenger seat.

Inside the shop Gwillym Parry was busy in the little cage in the corner which gave the Royal Stores all the dignity of a post office. He looked up from counting postal orders as the old-fashioned bell on the door jangled. He was a man of about fifty, with a craggy, lined face beneath a shock of grey hair. The strength of the face gave it a grandeur which was peculiarly Welsh. A native of Anglesey, he was the nearest thing to a close friend that Sandy had in the village. They played chess together, Gwillym usually winning. He had taught Sandy all he knew about fishing, and of the two of them he was the better educated, his parents having had the passion for education characteristic of the Welsh and the Scots. He could still construe Virgil or read the Welsh sagas in the mother tongue, which was more than Sandy could do.

The two men chatted easily, inconsequentially as old friends will. He agreed with May; apart from the engineer, there had been no strangers in the village.

They talked about the plans to flood the valley. Gwillym was on the local council, who were doing all they could to oppose the scheme.

'But they are so powerful, man,' he said. 'What can we do but talk for ever?'

Sandy asked for an ounce of tobacco. Gwillym got it from the shelf and turned back to the counter.

'Sandy, my father was a rockman. He died with the dust in his lungs. Silicosis they call it, but it's just the dust in the lungs. I bought this shop with the money my father saved – enough for the down-payment. Barley soup, we had. And six of us. Because the money had to go to the penny bank. If they build that dam . . . I'm a law-abiding man and a councillor, but if they build that dam, I'll be the first to cheer if Plaid Cymru blow it up.' His hand clenched on the tobacco so that what he handed to Sandy was far from a precise oblong.

Opposite the Royal Stores was the Maenofferen Arms, and as Sandy walked out of the shop, Evan Pritchard the landlord was standing in the doorway surveying the morning. He was wearing tweed trousers supported by red braces over a blue-striped shirt with no collar or tie. He was fat and he had clearly not shaved, and Sandy wondered for the five hundredth time why he disliked him so much. Despite the Welsh name, he was more English than Welsh, having spent most of his life east of the border.

'Morning, Evan,' Sandy called, concealing his dislike as he had so carefully done over the years.

'Morning, squire,' shouted the landlord. Sandy wondered why he so disliked being called 'squire'. He knew nothing against the landlord, except that he was fat and lazy and ran a squalid pub. But that was a charge that could be laid against many Welsh pubs. He made no use of his marvellous frontage overlooking the lake. Where there could have been a terrace or a garden there was a wilderness of nettles and junk which offended Sandy's orderly engineer's mind.

'Seen any visitors?' he asked. But Evan Pritchard only had an improbable story about three labourers from the 'dam electrics' who had tried to drink the 'yard of beer' hanging over the bar.

Welcomed by Pandy, he climbed back into the Land-Rover and drove past the few houses of the hamlet and along the margin of the lake. The lane deteriorated from rough tarmac to a couple of tarmac strips with grass and thistles growing between them. At the head of the lake the tarmac stopped altogether and there was only a rutted track full of stones and pot-holes so that the vehicle lurched and threw up sheets of muddy water.

He came at last to the Craig-y-Moch quarry and jerked to a halt by the roofless ruin of the quarrymen's barracks. As he clambered laboriously from the driving seat he saw the rain coming, a swirl across the lake. Then it was drenching him, soft, cold and penetrating – April in the Welsh hills. He turned up the collar of his jacket – a useless gesture as the sun vanished, the clouds clamped down and the rain came hissing like ten thousand snakes across the surface of the water.

Pandy, tail down, followed him into the ruined settlement. He stood a moment in the rain, considering. The barracks, the ruined chapel, the manager's house were almost blotted out by the rain. The stark incline which led into the quarry itself thrust upwards and disappeared in a swirl of cloud. There was no sound but the hiss of the rain, the drip and splash of water and the plaintive baaing of unseen sheep. He was very wet before he found what he was looking for – and then it was not altogether what he had expected. He found the remains of the fire in the graveyard of the chapel. It was on top of a slate tombstone close beneath the crumbling wall of the building. In the middle of the slate slab there was a mess of charred sticks and blackened ashes. The water was running across the slab, inky with the ashes, black against blue-grey, curling away from the remains of the fire and dripping like blood from the edge of the stone.

In the middle of the sodden remains of the fire there were charred bones, white bones, stark against the black of the charcoal. It was the burnt skeleton of a bird. There were draggled white feathers in the rank grass around the stone. Most of the flesh had been burnt from the skeleton, and sticking from the breastbone was something that looked like a cross – a slate cross, as if someone had made an obscene mockery of an Easter garden, using the bird's breast as the hill of Calvary.

Sandy had seen much horror in his service life. None the

14

less he had consciously to quell a shudder of revulsion as he plucked the cross from its resting place. He had to hold down the remains of the bird with one hand, a repulsive and messy business.

It was not a cross. It was a dagger, a slate dagger, simple in design, beautifully made, surprisingly sharp, and coming to a wicked point. A sinister and horrible thing.

Sandy dropped it into his pocket. He was suddenly aware of being wet and cold, of the overshadowing chapel wall, of the looming menace of the great hills. He limped back to the Land-Rover, and was grateful for the softness and warmth of Pandy's muzzle in his trailing hand.

2

Stranger in Hafod Maenen

The Reverend Septimus Treloar eased his pack from his shoulders, thereby allowing a further quarter pint of Welsh rainwater to trickle down his spine. He sat down, his back against a rock, the sodden turf soaking his behind. He cursed, fluently and comprehensively. He had been a Chief Inspector in the C.I.D. before he retired and became a clergyman, so he knew all the wrong phrases. First he cursed the romanticism, the idiotic desire to walk mountains again which had brought him from his flat fenland parish to the hills of North Wales. Next he cursed Mr Poucher's book, *The Welsh Peaks* which by promising him fine views of the Snowdon Horseshoe had brought him out on this particular lunatic jaunt. Not that it was Mr Poucher's fault — it was his own. Then he cursed

Welsh rain, mountains, bogs, and the mist that made all paths look the same. After that he cursed himself for his incompetence in getting lost. Finally, and for good measure, he just cursed. A woebegone sheep came out of the mist, saw him, and fled baaing.

'Bloody sheep,' said Septimus. A moment later his very ugly face creased into a grin. Then he started to laugh. Even the sheep thought he was round the twist, wandering about on top of a mountain on such an evening. He wiped the back of his hand across his streaming face and considered his position. The sad truth was that he was lost and it would be dark in an hour. He had no illusions. He had learned his mountaineering in the War – with partisans in Yugoslavia, and he was far too experienced to underestimate the seriousness of his position. On the other hand, because of his experience, he had followed all the proper mountain safety procedures and was equipped for a night in the open. He had extra clothing, food, whistle, torch, and even sufficient Polythene sheeting for a temporary bivouac. He had left his intended route with the landlord of the inn where he was staying, and they would know when to start worrying about him. Even so – and he forced himself to be realistic, knowing that Welsh mountains were not to be trifled with – he was miles off Poucher's route, he was no longer young, and a search party would do no manner of good fossicking around above Beddgellert when he was lost in the Moelwyns. Anyway – and he grinned again as the thought came to him – he would die of shame if he had to be rescued. It would get into the papers. 'Country Vicar in Helicopter Drama.' Sam Burroughs and all his old police colleagues would never let him forget it. A man only had to die once, and even death from exposure might be better than a collection of beefy young men from the R.A.F. Rescue trying to strap him on a stretcher. They would come with a chopper from Valley on Anglesey, and it would all cost the taxpayer a great deal of money. And the beefy young men would lecture him on the unwisdom of old fools who went blundering about on mountains when they ought to be dandling their grandchildren on their knees. Dammit! He *would* rather die of exposure! And anyway, he hadn't got any grandchildren – at least, not so far as he knew.

He got out map and compass, and Poucher's book, and started seriously to consider his position. He took a compass bearing – the sixth since he had realized he was lost. He guessed he must be close to the lake with the unpronounceable name Llyn-y-Moch. According to the map there were cliffs at one end – Craig-y-Moch. Of course, he had heard of them, though he had never climbed there. So that was how you pronounced the lake. Where the cliffs ended there was a disused slate quarry, various tracks running to it, and what looked like a sizable stream with 'Works' printed on the map where stream and lake joined. No doubt the stream had provided water power, and 'Works' would mark the site of the water-wheel.

He took his attention from the map and cocked his head on one side, listening. There was the crying of sheep, remote in the mist, the tinkle of the omnipresent water, and – yes! – far off, an indistinct roar. It could be the stream marked on the map. He heaved himself to his feet, picked up his pack and set off to investigate.

He found the stream twenty minutes later. Normally it would have been a typical mountain affair of small falls and pools – though the wise would have noted, even in high summer, the deep chasm it had cut for itself. This evening it was a roaring torrent of brown water and white foam. On the far side Septimus could see a track, a fisherman's path, running along the edge of the ravine, winding in and out of trees.

There was no crossing over, and Septimus, wise in the ways of mountains and streams, was cautious about following the torrent down the contours. 'I can think of better ways of breaking my neck,' he muttered, consulting the map again. However, the map indicated that the precipitous cliffs were on the far side of the stream, and that on his side the contours fell easily to the lake. He checked his compass bearing yet again, considered the approaching darkness, and decided he would have to risk it.

He set off down the mountainside, the stream a loud companion to his left. At first the going was fairly easy, patches of heather in turf close-cropped by the sheep. Then there was a patch of gorse which tore at his clothing. Then the slope steepened, and the ground began to fall away in rough steps, a natural staircase for a giant, with granite risers and treads of boggy grass. More than once he went in over his ankles, and once he nearly pitched headlong over a six-foot drop. He paused, cleaning his boots with a piece of stone, and then went on more cautiously. He had to start using his torch to find where to put his feet, to ensure that he was not about to clamber over a precipice.

The natural steps came to an end, and he stumbled through a field of breast-high bracken, its roots snatching at his feet, its fronds soaking the scant remainder of him that was still dry. After the bracken he came to trees. They were bounded by a dry-stone wall which he welcomed as the first sign of civilization.

It was dark and dripping in the wood, and the tree roots seemed intent on tripping him. He had to use the torch all the time now, for the last of the daylight had gone, and the wood falling away below him was black with the total darkness of the Pit.

No. Not total darkness. To his left where the stream clamoured in its fissure there was a red light, indistinct in the rain, a glow like that of an autumn bonfire. He could see the smoke rising grey above the glow, and the twisted shapes of the trees silhouetted, black against red. Curious, he switched off his torch and moved towards the glow. He came through the trees to the edge of the ravine. Unseen, forty, sixty or a hundred feet below the stream roared down its rocky course. All the far bank was dark, the trees merging with the night so

18

that it was difficult to distinguish the one from the other. The fire seemed all the brighter for the surrounding darkness, a fire with a halo of red and orange, fading to yellow and merging with the mist. It seemed to rise from a pinnacle of rock on the far bank, and as Septimus watched there was the shadow of a man, dark like a bat, stooping over it. Then suddenly the fire vanished as if it had been extinguished with water, and there was only darkness and the roar of the torrent.

Half an hour later he came out of the wood and out of the cloud. Below him stretched the lake, a road running round its upper end, while across it the lights of a village bade him welcome. It took him a further half-hour to trudge round the end of the lake, but at last, footsore and very tired, he reached the village. It was hardly a village, just a handful of houses clustered round what looked like a water mill, a village shop, and – glory be! – on the edge of the lake, a pub. The Mae-nofferen Arms.

Septimus threw open the door of the bar and marched in, conscious of his squelching boots and bedraggled appearance, feeling as if he was a visitor from outer space. The soft conversation of a dozen Welsh voices was suddenly cut off as the door crashed melodramatically behind him. His policeman's mind noted that like most Welsh pub doors, the damping cylinder on the closing device was broken. They looked at him as he stood dripping Welsh water on to worn Welsh lino; four men playing dominoes, illegal money on the table beside them; two playing darts; a courting couple in the corner; a handsome, middle-aged man with a shock of grey hair sitting by the coal fire and smoking a pipe; and a rather bedraggled young man with long hair and a doubtful beard leaning against the bar.

The dramatic pause lasted for perhaps three seconds, then the illicit dominoes, the darts, the soft voices started again. The man with the grey hair took his pipe from his mouth and said, 'Good evening. You have had a wet day for walking.'

Septimus smiled and agreed, taking off his battered tweed hat, shaking it first, and then wringing the water out of it, aware of the water streaming off his person, the pool spreading round his feet. He was amused. Apart from the man with the grey hair, the other regulars in the bar were so obviously pretending not to notice the cuckoo in the nest. He had a sudden urge to shout, 'I am a Dalek, Exterminate! Exterminate!' Or he could try the classic phrase, 'Take me to your leader', or point his walking-stick at the hairy young man as if it were some unimaginably destructive laser gun. He contained his adolescent impulses, squelched to the bar, eased his pack to the floor, said 'Good evening' to the hairy young man, was ostentatiously ignored, wiped his face with a grubby handkerchief, and was just in time to greet the landlord who appeared suddenly, like a pantomime demon, through a dubious and greasy curtain.

'Evening, landlord. I'll have a double whisky.' He looked at the inverted bottles at the back of the bar. 'Teachers. No. On second thoughts, make it a treble whisky.'

'Hiking then?' The landlord was busy with glass and spirit measure, his back to Septimus. A fat man, wearing a striped shirt and no collar. Septimus considered. He disliked the rear view of the landlord – the rolls of fat, the superfluous stud in the neck band of the shirt, the straining red braces. The man might at least pay his customers the courtesy of washing his neck and wearing a collar! And why did he dislike the word 'hiking' so much? It made him feel like an antediluvian Boy Scout, Baden-Powell hat, knobbly knees and long shorts. 'We'll dib-dib-dib, we'll dob-dob-dob . . .' No. That was Cubs.

'You could say that,' he replied. He took his whisky and poured water from the jug on the bar. 'Have you got a phone I could use, landlord?'

The man grinned – not a pleasant expression. He spoke as if he had achieved some sort of victory. 'No phone, mister. This isn't Birmingham, you know. There's a public box over the road. If it's working that is – if the tearaways from Blaenau

20

Ffestiniog haven't done it over. Last time was when they lost to Portmadoc. Football, in case you don't know.'

He giggled as if he had said something clever. Septimus wondered, as he had often done before, why it was that some publicans seemed to take a perverse delight in being unpleasant to their customers. He must remember to ask Charlie, the landlord of the Bluebell, about it when he got back home. The long-haired young man turned and spoke. Up to that point – as Septimus had noticed with the enquiring part of his mind that was never entirely quiescent – the broad rejection of the turned back had been very obvious. As the young man turned Septimus looked squarely at him. Their eyes met a moment, blue and guileless looking into deep-set brown in a sensitive face framed by the long hair and the adolescent beard. The young man shifted his gaze and spoke a few sentences in liquid Welsh. The landlord laughed. Septimus noted the false heartiness.

'You won't know the Welsh, Mister. Dylan says the phone is wrecked and someone has written up "bugger the English".'

The obvious reply to that was 'bugger the Welsh', but Septimus was a pacific man and so opted for the ambiguous murmur, 'What an exhausting task.'

The nonplussed silence which this produced was broken by the grey-headed man by the fire. He had taken his pipe from his mouth and was pointing with it. It was an educated voice, and it was angry, its Welsh lilt reminding Septimus of the mountains from which he had just come.

'Dylan Wesley Jones you ought to be ashamed of yourself, using that language in a public place, to a stranger who has done you no manner of harm, and your father a deacon, and a respected member of the community.'

Darts stopped, dominoes stopped, and the secret exchanges of the courting couple. The bar clientele were hanging on the eloquence of the grey-headed man.

'A musical nation,' thought Septimus inconsequentially, 'Much given to singing flat and talking at length.'

'If you were my son I would belt you, big though you are. And if you, Evan Pritchard, knew your job and had respect for a visitor, you would turn him out of this bar parlour. If the phone outside the shop is out of order, why cannot you tell the gentleman in courtesy and English, which you speak as well as your mother tongue? Where is your hospitality, man, for someone who has been walking the mountains? Where is your good manners that your mother, God rest her, taught you?' The grey-headed man was on his feet now, coming towards the bar.

Dylan, his face red with shame, said something angry in Welsh, was answered sharply in the same way, and slammed out of the bar.

There was a moment of silence, then the dominoes, the darts and the lilting voices started again. The brief drama was over.

'Sorry about that,' said the grey-headed man, putting his drink down on the bar. 'I must apologize for Dylan who is the son of a friend of mine. He had no cause to insult you.'

Septimus grinned. He had been sworn at far too often to be in the least put out. 'No harm done. I didn't understand his insults anyway. Name of Septimus Treloar.' He thrust out a big hand.

'Gwillym Parry. I keep the shop across the road. You can use my phone and welcome.'

'Thanks very much,' said Septimus. 'I'd be most grateful. My landlord'll be thinking I'm lost on the Glyders. Get out the R.A.F. Rescue I shouldn't wonder. Have a drink.' There was a pause while the fat landlord, much chastened by Gwillym's fierceness, poured the drinks.

'Young Dylan,' said Septimus, 'he's a Welsh Nationalist, I suppose? Doesn't like the English?'

'You could say that. But there's Plaid Cymru and Plaid Cymru. I'm a Nationalist myself.'

'So would I be,' said Septimus, 'if I was a Welshman. Actually I'm Cornish. Might be blowing up Princetown or

22

squatting in a caravan park if I still lived at home. But then I don't. I live in East Anglia, and I've never heard of the Free Norfolk Army.'

Gwillym smiled. 'It is a question of proportion, Mr Treloar. Dylan got rusticated from Bangor University over a plan to throw eggs at the Prince of Wales.' He saw Septimus's look of startled interest and added, 'Oh, only a plan. They never threw them. They had the eggs. Hundreds, man. Mostly bad. Proper magazine of them. But what I say is, what harm has the young man done to Wales? Steering ships and going to church. Innocent activity I call it, and he has at least tried to learn the language, though I shouldn't think he can be very intelligible, not after only a year. But then we are all a bit touched in this village on account of the plan to dam the valley and turn the llyn into a reservoir. Lose our homes.'

'I'm sorry,' said Septimus. 'I didn't know. Tell me about it.'

'Nothing to tell really. Just what I said. They are working at the end of the valley now. Taking soundings to see if the rock is firm enough for a dam.'

'And you can only hope it isn't, I suppose?' said Septimus.

'We do what we can. But it is all so unfair. Using our own money that they take in taxes to employ counsel to make us look fools in court, while we run jumble sales to pay our lawyers. Perhaps you can excuse Dylan for being bitter. His family has been turned out once before when they made Llyn Celyn. But you will have seen in the papers that someone threw their tools into the lake. And there was a bomb that did not go off. I am opposed to bombs, but I must confess I did smile a little.'

Septimus was conscious of the conflict in his imagination, his natural sympathy with the underdog at war with his policeman's disapproval of violence.

'And was that young Dylan?' he asked.

'Nobody said so, man. But I shouldn't be surprised.'

23

Septimus was pondering the extraordinary way allegations of serious crime could be bandied between total strangers when the bar door opened. He looked round as the door produced its unmelodious clank.

The man who came in was about the same age as Septimus, heavily built, wearing a fawn duffle coat and a battered felt hat.

Septimus automatically registered 'retired army officer' before he diagnosed the limp as an artificial leg and looked up at the square face with its grizzled military moustache. He took perhaps half a second to readjust his reactions.

'Hullo, Sandy,' he said. 'Long time no see.'

The Colonel stopped in mid march in the centre of the silence in the bar. With quiet amusement Septimus watched the play of emotions over the soldier's face, the groping in the past, the grin of dawning recognition.

'Good God! Septimus.' He came quickly forward, almost falling on the big priest in his haste and delight. Septimus noted the clumsy movements with a sharp pang of memory – quick as a flashlight photograph – Major Sanderson rolling up a parachute beside a railway bridge in the Yugoslavian sunlight.

'Have a drink, old son,' he said. 'I take it you know Mr Parry?'

The bar parlour resumed its activities. Two old friends had met. That was one of the purposes of bar parlours.

'A brandy,' said Sandy, and then to Gwillym, 'Last time I saw this old so-and-so, I'd just jumped out of an aeroplane. It's . . . thirty years, Septimus.'

'The Hjoda railway bridge wasn't the last time,' said Septimus, fumbling with change, 'last time was when we put you on that train all dressed up like an engine driver, and the girl at the bookstall swore you were her husband.'

'So she did! I never understood why the police believed her. And you were pretending to be Tito's A.D.C. Remember that daft uniform?'

'All gold braid and fancy buttons,' agreed Septimus.

'Just like a commissionaire at a cinema.' They hugged each other and laughed aloud, like two children remembering a successful piece of mischief, unaware of the Welsh bar in their sharp memories of shared danger.

Half an hour later Septimus was leaning back in a leather armchair in the Mill sitting-room, his feet stretched out to the log fire. He had used Sandy's phone to stave off the impending rescue operation and to make arrangements about his Land-Rover. He was wearing a roll-neck sweater out of his pack and a pair of Sandy's trousers which were too short for him, and a shabby pair of Sandy's slippers which fitted tolerably well. He was dry, warm, comfortable and inclined to be sleepy.

They had swapped stories, filling in the gaps, and now they came to a silence. They listened to the spit and crackle of the fire and the occasional brush of rain on the window.

Sandy stirred restlessly, got up and went to the window. Septimus, lying nearly horizontal in the deep chair, opened one eye.

'Expecting someone?'

For answer Sandy went to his desk and took out the slate dagger.

'What do you make of that?'

Septimus turned it over in his big hands. It was a beautifully made thing, but a wicked thing. A dagger and a parody of a cross.

'It's been in a fire,' he said.

'Yes.'

'There are stains on it. They're burnt on to the slate. Blood?'

'Yes.'

'It's sharp. You could do someone a mischief with this. Probably snap in the wound. Nasty.'

'What do you make of it?'

25

'Masterpiece of a slatemaker's apprentice. Little brother cut himself with it. Mum threw it on the kitchen fire in a rage. English colonel rescued it from the flames as a genuine Welsh *objet d'art*. Anything else I can tell you, Watson?' He held out the dagger to Sandy.

'You got it all wrong.'

'You tell me, then.'

Sandy told the story, and despite himself, Septimus was intrigued. He told Sandy about the fire he had seen as he had come down the mountainside. Very odd. Midnight bonfires? Sacrificial fires at the witching hour? Who would wish to slaughter, apparently to sacrifice, a seabird on a tombstone in the derelict graveyard of a ruined church at three o'clock in the morning?

'Fricasseeing chickens in churchyards,' he said. 'You want a trick cyclist, not a parson.'

'Not a chicken,' said Sandy, 'and I think it needs a policeman, not a psychiatrist.'

Septimus chose to ignore the obvious reference to himself. 'Why a copper?'

The old soldier paused before replying. Septimus could see the look of bewildered distaste on his bluff, honest face.

'It seems so . . . so – barbaric,' he said at length.

Barbaric. That, Septimus reflected, was exactly the right word. In his colourful life he had seen many cruelties – gang beatings, murders, rapes, psychopathic attacks, but never anything so – precisely – barbaric. It smacked of nameless rites from the pre-Christian dark ages. A Bible phrase came into his mind, 'Children passing through the fire to Moloch.'

'So you need a copper?' he said.

Sandy looked down at him, the frosty gleam of military command hardening in his grey eyes. 'You are a policeman.'

'I'm not,' replied Septimus firmly. 'I'm an antiquated country parson on a walking holiday, and I don't want to get involved with local layabouts, villains, or Taffy acting like a psychopathic nut-case. Anyway, it's a job for the local fuzz.'

'They call our local Dai Truncheon,' said Sandy, the frosty gleam still in his eye, 'and he couldn't detect a simple case of Sunday opening – not if they were singing *Sospan Fach* at the top of their voices in the bar parlour. Anyway, it did happen in a churchyard. Doesn't that make it your business?'

'Not tonight it doesn't,' said Septimus firmly as he heaved himself to his feet. 'I've been squelching over Welsh bog since nine this morning, and I'm for my bed.'

Sandy's grin melted the frost of military command. 'Good. We'll go and view the scene of the crime in the morning.'

'Damn your eyes,' said Septimus and stumped up the stairs.

Half an hour and a hot bath later Septimus was sitting in his bedroom in a pair of Sandy's pyjamas. He had extracted a rather damp Office Book from his pack, and was saying Evensong without much attention. Like Macbeth, he could see a phantom dagger before his eyes. He tossed the Office Book on to the bed and went to the window. The rain had stopped for the moment, but the cloud was low over the mountains, and the scattered lights of the village were ghostly yellow, as if in a London fog. Across the lake all was dark.

Confound Sandy and his squalid little mystery! Yobboes playing at witches. But was it more than that? And where had they come from? If Sandy was to be believed, not through the village. And how did you trap a seagull? And where had the hypothetical yobbo got the dagger?

Made it, presumably – and not for bovver at the Criccieth football match. Then there was the fire which he had seen himself. Probably unconnected, but very odd none the less.

He looked into the blackness over the lake where the mountains guarded their secrets under the clouds and the immemorial mists. To go out there, miles from anywhere, and sacrifice a bird on a tombstone in a ruined churchyard by a derelict quarry – in the name of God – why? He shrugged, drew the curtains and went to bed.

3

Hugh-ap-Lloyd's Altar

'There's nothing to investigate. And if there is, it's Dai Truncheon's job. I'm not a policeman, I'm a parson. A parson on holiday. Your local villains can sacrifice *maidens* for all I care.' Septimus was sitting at the kitchen table, and Sandy, in dressing-gown, stood at the cooker in an aroma of bacon and egg. It was May Parry's morning off.

'Suit yourself,' said Sandy over the noise of frying.

Septimus said nothing. He merely felt more irritated. He had emerged from Sandy's spare bed, stiff, sleepy and cross, like a disgruntled grizzly coming out of hibernation. He helped himself to coffee. He had surveyed his ugly unshaven face in the mirror with considerable distaste. 'You', he had said to his mirror image, 'will have nothing to do with this ridiculous lark.' The mirror image had nodded solemn agreement. He had set about his whiskers with Sandy's razor in a mood of firm resolve.

The coffee was jolly good. He helped himself to cornflakes.

The pages of his Office Book had been stuck together with damp – damned Welsh water – and the matins Old Testament lesson had been about Jephthah sacrificing his daughter, which was clearly a deep-laid plot by the compilers of the lectionary. Like a sunbeam over ice floes, a gleam of laughter stole over his mind.

'Watch the plate, it's hot.' Sandy removed his cornflakes bowl and dropped bacon and eggs in front of him. Septimus realized he was hungry. He remembered C.I.D. lectures of long ago. Who has been killed? When and where, and how and why? He cut rind off bacon and put up an imaginary cadet hand. 'Please sir, a seagull at 03.15 last Tuesday. With a slate dagger. On a tombstone in the ruins of a pre-Reformation chapel.' The bacon was very good. So was the egg.

'Sandy,' he asked, 'whose was the tombstone?' The colonel looked up from pouring coffee.

'Search me. I never looked. Should I have?'

'Very careless of you,' said Septimus. 'After breakfast we shall go and see.'

It was a great blue-black oblong of unadorned slate standing alone by the broken wall of the ruined chancel. Beyond the churchyard wall the land fell gently to the lake. Half a mile away, and almost opposite, was the Mill. Septimus dragged out a handful of rank grass and swept away the repulsive litter of burnt bones, feathers and blackened sticks. There was an inscription, brief to the point of abruptness.

Huw-ap-Llwyd
1732
Pregethwr
Cyntaf Samuel 28;13

'Llwyd is the Welsh for Lloyd,' said Sandy.

'And what does *pregethwr* mean?' asked Septimus. 'Perhaps he was the Rev Hugh-ap-Lloyd. Presumably the last bit is a Bible reference.'

'He may have been a parson,' said Sandy. 'At least he's got an altar up in the hills.'

'An altar?'

'That's what they call it. Hugh-ap-Lloyd's altar. It's a great rock, a column really, in the middle of the stream. He's supposed to have stood on it and preached.'

'Stood on his altar?' said Septimus. 'He must have been a

very odd clergyman. Anyway, Welsh preachers don't hold with altars do they?'

'You'll have to ask John Wesley Jones about it,' said Sandy, 'Dylan's father. He's our local history boffin.'

'I'll do that,' Septimus replied. 'But for now I'd like to have a look at Mr Lloyd's altar. Can you show me?'

'With my timber leg?' said Sandy. 'I'll wait here for you.' He pointed with his stick to where the green ravine of the stream came precipitously down the mountainside. 'There's a fisherman's path on the far side. You'll know the altar when you get there. Take you about twenty minutes.'

Septimus set off, his feet jingling broken slate. Sandy shouted after him, 'Won't do you any good. You can't get on to it.'

Septimus struggled up the incline past the buildings and the piles of slate spoil, skirted the edge of the quarry and plunged into trees. The path climbed steeply so that sometimes he had to use his hands. It wound among the trees, around rocks, sometimes along the edge of the ravine, sometimes moving away. As he moved upwards the valley narrowed and the stream became a series of deep pools and thundering falls, the pools gouged out like cauldrons, the falls spouting torrents which roared around rocks, over rocks, between and under rocks.

There was no missing Hugh-ap-Lloyd's altar. It was a geological freak of the first order. Or as Septimus, who was sensitive to atmosphere, told himself, it was like the pillar of some wicked magician planted by black art in the middle of the ravine, a secret place and charged with danger. It was a column of rock rising some seventy feet out of the water, higher than the sides of the ravine. On three sides it was almost sheer, but on the downstream side it went down in massive, uneven steps like a giant staircase. The top was roughly oblong so that it did look like an altar. Septimus stood and gazed at it, his chest heaving. It was dark among the trees, and there was no sound but the clamour of the water.

'Well, no one would have heard his sermon anyway,' said Septimus to himself.

And to whom had he preached? The trout – a sort of Welsh Saint Francis? And how on earth had he got to his altar? Perhaps he really had been a wizard and had flown there. Septimus moved cautiously to the edge of the ravine and peered into the clamorous depths. It was an awesome place, and to fall would be certain death. About six feet down the cliff a fir tree – one of many clinging to the sides of the ravine like survivors from a shipwreck – had fallen across the chasm, its top lodged on the staircase side of the pulpit rock. Well . . . there was nothing remarkable about that. In the unending, silent struggle of nature plenty of trees died and fell across ravines. He had seen at least three on his way up. Only this was not a dead tree. It grew from a narrow ledge, and its splintered top where it rested on the pinnacle of rock was still green. It looked an easy climb down to the ledge. There were plenty of handholds, and if he did slip the ledge itself would hold him. He turned and dangled his feet over the edge, taking a secure anchorage with his left hand on a rocky projection, and started to climb down.

Perhaps it was the thunder of the stream in the enclosed space which made rational thought difficult, or – as Septimus always maintained afterwards – perhaps there really was an evil magic about the place. Certainly he was acting out of character. Normally he was far too wise to take such a risk without a rope and a secure belay. Whatever the reason, he simply forgot that the earth and undergrowth in such a rocky and precipitous place would be a mere coating, like the skin on custard, like a rug on a slippery floor. He reached down with his foot . . . and gently as a blessing, everything gave way beneath his hands and feet. It was as if the whole ravine side was sliding inexorably into the boiling death sixty feet below. The movement was so slow that he had time to think. A kaleidoscope of images flashed like the frames of a film strip across his mind, even as he saw the naked rock where his left hand had seemed so secure. A fight outside an East End pub. A riot during the General Strike. Bullets skipping off a pavement. A cave in Yugoslavia. 'God!' he thought, 'What a stupid way to die.' Then, his deep faith coming to his aid, 'Lord Jesus, receive my soul.' There was a wild moment when everything seemed to be sliding, and then a sudden, blessed stillness. Winded, he lay in a tangle of broken brambles, damp moss and dead leaves on the ledge from which the pine tree grew, his head over the edge so that he was looking down into the boiling cauldron of the stream fifty feet below. Convulsively he jerked back, and everything stirred and slid three inches nearer to death. He lay still, trying for the moment by sheer will-power to stop all movement from his own pulse to the precession of the equinox.

So he hung between life and death, whether for minutes or seconds or that eternity which is called a split second, only the Recording Angel can tell. A dipper landed on the roots of the fir tree. It bobbed twice, its black and white breast making it look like a bowing waiter, then it fled with a thin cry of alarm. From his shoulder blades Septimus could tell that the ledge was a fraud, a mere slope of rock which over the years had gathered enough vegetation to make promises which, like a whore, it could not fulfil. If he moved the whole lot would go over the edge, and that would be that. And he wasn't even sure that there was an after-life, though he had laid his bets on the possibility. It seemed very likely that he would soon know. It had been a good life, a full life, not so far off the Biblical span. The Cornish childhood with the empty cliffs and beaches, and London and the camaraderie of the Force, and the crimes he had solved or failed to solve. The girl he had loved but not married, and the friendships. Sam Burroughs would certainly investigate his death, and come to the sad conclusion that he had simply fallen over the edge, an appalling idea. A half-formed thought came into his mind: 'I'm not a bloody tourist in beach sandals and shorts.' He spoke aloud, 'Come on, Septimus, let's try and be intelligent.'

Screwing down panic like the safety valve on some leaky old boiler, he considered his position, firmly refusing to look down. He was half over the edge and held by nothing but brambles as tenacious as they were treacherous, but just beyond his bent knees was the trunk of the pine tree. That at least must be fairly firm. With infinite caution he extracted his knife from his trouser pocket. Perversely, for no apparent reason, his insubstantial mattress slid a further two inches. He closed his eyes. The movement stopped. He opened his eyes again, and opened the knife, ignoring the danger, trying to calculate as coldly as possible which brambles he must cut to give him the chance of life, which must be left to hold him on the ledge which was no ledge.

He made his decisions and cut the chosen strands. 'Here goes,' he said, and flung himself towards the fir tree. His fingers scrabbled on bark and damp earth even as the mess of brambles and rotting leaves slid from beneath his feet and over the edge. Such was the clamour of the stream that there was no sound of its going. But it was all right, his grip on the roots of the pine was secure. Carefully he hauled himself up and inched himself into the hollow where the roots had torn from the ravine side, waiting for his trembling to stop, for his breathing to come back to normal.

Then he saw that the whole episode had been quite unnecessary. On the far side of the fir, solid rock climbed up the ravine side in a series of easy steps.

'Well, I'll be damned,' he said. 'Time I gave up playing at Batman and used what little brain I've got.'

There were footmarks in the soft mould on top of the steps, the chevron pattern of a heavy rubber sole – wellingtons, or rubber-soled walking boots. What was more, there were muddy marks on the trunk of the fir. He picked a piece of compacted mud from the wood. It had come from the chevron pattern of a boot sole. Had someone really stood up on that trunk and walked across that terrible ravine to Hugh-ap-Lloyd's altar? He looked down and shuddered. He supposed it could be done. He supposed he could do it himself if he had the Wrath of God snapping at his heels. But he wasn't going to do it – not to investigate the murder of a seagull.

His attention was caught by a sprinkling of what looked like white powder. It was lying in the cavity where the roots of the tree had pulled away from the cliff. He took a pinch of it, rubbing it between finger and thumb, putting it to his nostrils. It was sawdust. He forgot his fears in a surge of curiosity. Two of the roots had not pulled out, they had been sawn through. So someone had felled the fir tree to make a bridge. Now entirely in the power of his curiosity Septimus got to his feet and tested the security of the trunk. It seemed firm enough. As a bridge its only limitation was its horrifying narrowness. He threw a leg over the trunk and sat astride it, considering. Someone had sacrificed a seabird on Hugh-ap-Lloyd's tomb. Someone – the same someone? – had made a bridge to Hugh-ap-Lloyd's altar. He greatly desired to know whether there was any connection. He looked down . . . and looked up again. Refusing to consider the rationality of what he was about to do he commended himself into the hands of God, fixed his eyes on the shattered tip of the fir and started to hutch across.

In a way it was not too bad. At least the trunk seemed comfortingly solid, and he resisted the temptation to glance down. The worst moment was when his trouser leg caught on the stub of a branch and he had to extract his knife and laboriously cut the stub off, and below the knife blade he could see the rocks and the swirling water at the bottom of the ravine. He got to the far side with nothing worse than another rent in his already ruined trousers, and a long scratch on the inside of his thigh.

Thankfully he struggled out of the broken tree top. He was on the altar itself.

The rock was perhaps twenty feet across – wider than it

looked from the side of the ravine. There were footprints plain to see in the coarse grass. He followed them round the top of the tree and down the rock. It was an easy scramble apart from the slippery surface and the hungry water below. About twenty feet down there was a wide, flat ledge above a sheer drop into the black pool. It was an awful place. It was dark, for trees and rock closed overhead so that it was hardly possible to see the blessed sky. Below was the swirling pool, like the cauldron of some giant witch whose evil magic had turned the bright water of the mountain stream into a hell brew flecked with yellow scum. The noise numbed the brain. Confined by the narrow canyon the roar of the fall hammered unendingly on the ears, and the spray blew bitterly cold, a swirling cloud wetter than heavy rain.

Septimus looked down. How deep was the pool? He had no means of telling. He had a surrealist vision of it going down for ever into the darkness under the earth, its black caves the lurking places of vast and nameless monsters. His conscious mind told him that it was nothing but a deep pool in a mountain torrent, his subconscious knew it to be a place of great evil. Certainly no one who fell into it would have the slightest chance of coming out alive. As if to confirm the thought, something grey rolled to the surface where the fall thundered into the pool.

A drowned sheep. It rolled on to its back, floating free from the fall, its four legs stuck pathetically in the air and tossing as if it were struggling to turn over. The current caught it and it was drawn – terrifyingly swiftly – towards the side where the rock was scoured, round and smooth. Then, as if seized by the tentacles of some nightmare octopus, it vanished beneath the surface, and Septimus saw it no more.

There was no vegetation on the ledge where he was standing. It was bare rock, and had it not been so rough it would have been desperately slippery. His policeman's mind noted that it would take no footprints. Even so, there were clear signs of his predecessor. A Players No 6 cigarette carton, a plastic envelope which had once contained fishing hooks, and – fallen into a crevice in the rock – a small oblong of lead with a hole punched in it.

Septimus looked glumly at the trophies in the palm of his hand, then the imp of self-mockery took charge. He had risked life and limb on this lunatic goose-chase following the trail of a mad Welshman, half angler, half goat. A mad Welshman who – if he had not done so already – richly deserved to drown.

He pocketed the trophies and cautiously retraced his steps. He got back to the tree, and there was another set of tracks leading upward to the top of the altar. He followed, using his hands to scramble up the last six feet until he was standing on the highest step, the summit of the pillar level with his waist.

It was indeed an altar.

The top was flat, a regular rectangle which had been squared and smoothed with tools. Around the edge, like the inlay on a table, a band of decoration had been carved. The stone was too eroded to tell what the decoration had been. In the centre of the rectangle, lying amid the blackened ends of charred sticks were the half-burnt remains of a fish, a trout about fifteen inches long. Sticking from the remains of the rib cage was a slate dagger.

4

A Stone in the Night

Septimus could see Sandy far below him, his balding head
standing out, a tiny white dot in a field of blue and grey. He
was sitting on the remains of the churchyard wall and there
was another man with him. The priest clattered on to the top
of the steep incline. 'Oy!' he shouted, waving. Sandy looked
up and waved back and came limping through the rank grass
to greet Septimus at the bottom of the incline.

'Septimus, I want to introduce . . . Ye gods and little
apples! What have you been up to?'

Septimus was nonplussed.

'You look like Johnny-down-the-pit.'

Absently Septimus detached a fair length of bramble from
the wreck of his jacket. There was a tear in his trousers expos-
ing pink thigh. His beloved old suit would have to go into the
dustbin. He was very muddy.

'I had a fall,' he said mildly.

Sandy made a noise uncommonly like a snort. 'Fall! You've
got half the Moelwyns plastered across your face, and those
trousers are not decent.' Septimus pulled out a handkerchief
and started to scrub at his face. This merely made matters
worse.

Sandy turned to the stranger who had waited silently during this exchange. A tall man with greying hair and a big-
boned face.

'John. This is my friend Septimus. The Reverend Septimus

Treloar. He's an Anglican parson, though you wouldn't think it to look at him. John Wesley Jones.'

'I feel more like a hedge priest,' said Septimus taking the proffered hand, his innocent blue eyes meeting those of the Welshman, dark eyes with a hint of hidden fire. Instinctively the two men liked each other.

'Sandy was telling me about you,' said Septimus easily, 'the resident expert on local history.'

The Welshman smiled, warm and welcoming. 'I know a little. But man! You do not want to be falling in the afon. It is a dangerous place.'

'So I discovered,' replied Septimus.

'And you found the old wizard's pillar, did you?'

'Yes,' Septimus said, 'and I've been on to it.'

He enjoyed the Welshman's reaction, wonder chasing disbelief and astonishment across his face. He explained about the tree, being careful to say nothing about the cut roots, or the dead fish.

'You have been on to Hugh-ap-Lloyd's altar? You have done something few locals have done. Not many have stood where Hugh stood. And what did you find there?' Was it Septimus's imagination, or was there a hint of anxiety in the question? His caution working overtime, he drew from his pocket the cigarette packet, the envelope and the piece of lead. He could feel the slate dagger cold and smooth against the back of his hand.

'Someone had been fishing.'

Wesley Jones looked at the trophies, and then nodded. A pontifical nod, like a decision in a deacons' meeting in chapel.

'Sheep Shechem,' he said. 'Sheep Shechem smokes those when he can afford them, and he is crazy enough to fish from the altar. A great fisherman. He worms for trout – and salmon when the bailiff is not looking. Makes his own weights. Steals the lead from the chapel roof. Mostly he smokes clover. And a very foul smell it is, too.'

'So you'd opt for Mr Shechem?' said Septimus.

'Sheep Shechem is mad enough to walk across the afon on a fir for the sake of catching a trout.'

Septimus noted the reference to a fir. He had not said what the tree was. 'He's got a very strange name,' he said, 'Sheep Shechem.'

The other man smiled. 'Sheep Shechem is not his real name. Honestly, I do not know what his real name is. I do not suppose he knows himself. He lives with his mother on the other side of the hill.'

'You say he's mad,' said Septimus. 'Just about fishing – or in other ways?' Wesley Jones' face changed. Was it sorrow, or was it caution? Septimus could not say.

'Sheep Shechem,' said Wesley Jones, choosing his words carefully, 'is both very gentle and very dangerous. Sick animals . . . and he is like Saint Francis. But strangers, people he does not trust . . .? He nearly killed a Council official who tried to move him and his mother out of their cottage. He lives in his own world and anything that comes from outside is a danger.'

'Is he educated?' Septimus asked.

'I should not think he can read, if that is what you mean by education.'

'But would he know – understand – whatever stories there are?'

'Stories?' the Welshman asked.

'About Hugh-ap-Lloyd, for instance.'

'He would know some of them – but not truly, not as they exist in the old records. But many of the stories have been told from mouth to mouth. Much garbled, they are, in the telling. But Sheep Shechem on the altar . . .?' Wesley Jones paused and shook his head. 'Certainly he would fish from the altar, and it would not surprise me if he believed that he could talk with Hugh-ap-Lloyd himself. It is an awesome place.'

With this, Septimus could only agree. 'What do you think he might talk about?' he asked.

'I do not know what goes on in Sheep Shechem's mind,'

replied the Welshman, 'but he might talk of the things that frighten him, the things that he hates, that are happening to the valleys he loves.' He broke off suddenly and called, 'Gwyn! Gwyn!'

A little boy came round the side of the derelict cottages. His white hair reminded Septimus of the Saxon children of his own East coast parish.

Wesley Jones stooped to the little boy and spoke in Welsh. The two Englishmen watched, Septimus aware of himself as an alien. 'Taffy was a Welshman,' he thought, 'and Taffy was . . .' well – what? A man whose country had been over-run all those years ago by the arrogant English. A man who clung tenaciously to the secrets of rock and mountain, the singing of streams musical as his own tongue. He did not know what Taffy was, and he was humble enough to recognize his own ignorance. Wesley Jones took the little boy by the hand and gravely introduced him to Septimus.

The little boy looked up at the battered adult face, his head tilted back, then he turned to Wesley Jones and spoke in Welsh. Wesley Jones translated.

'He says if you are a minister, you ought to have a Bible, and why are your trousers torn?'

Septimus dropped to his haunches and took Gwyn's hands. 'I've left my Bible at Colonel Sandy's, and I tore my trousers because I fell in a bramble bush.'

The child nodded solemnly, entirely satisfied with the explanation.

'Come along, Gwyn bach,' said Wesley Jones, 'we have all the slates to load and we must get you home in time for dinner.' He took Gwyn by the hand and they moved away through the tombstones. By the wall he stopped.

'Mr Treloar, the Colonel says you want to know about Hugh-ap-Lloyd.' Septimus agreed. 'Come to my house tonight. About eight o'clock? And we will talk.'

Septimus watched as the man and the boy disappeared hand in hand into the quarry.

'I thought that quarry was derelict,' he said.

'It is – more or less,' Sandy replied, 'but there's still worth-while slate in the tips so the Company sends John up here when he has nothing else to do. Makes small slates – damp courses and so on.' He looked curiously at Septimus. 'Come on, old son, what have you been up to – apart from rolling in the brambles?'

Septimus handed him the slate dagger. 'Hugh-ap-Lloyd's got an altar on that rock – a real one. And someone sacrificed a trout on it. Could have been last night. It's about where I saw the fire.'

'Sheep Shechem?' said Sandy.

'Could well be,' Septimus replied. 'But what on earth for?'

Sandy shrugged, examining the dagger. 'We're all a bit touched,' he said, 'on account of what May calls the dam electrics. After all, you've got me worrying about fires in the night, and Gwillym Parry hoping Plaid Cymru will blow it up. What Sheep Shechem might do, I wouldn't know. You heard what John said – he could hardly be described as a stable character.'

Septimus repeated himself. 'But what on earth for? Dam electrics and sacrificing birds and fish?'

Sandy looked hard at his friend, and his face was very grave. 'If you'd lived here as long as I have,' he said, 'no-thing would surprise you.'

He handed the dagger back to Septimus. 'It's the same as the other, only bigger,' he said. They both looked at the thing in silence. Slate of the mountains and a parody of the cross of Christ. For all its fine workmanship, it seemed an evil thing.

Sandy was looking out of the window of the Mill sitting-room. The lake was very calm, reflecting on its surface the jagged line of the high hills. The hills were black with the coming night and edged with a bright green line where the sun had gone down behind Moelwyn Mawr. He drew the curtains and limped across to throw a log on the fire. A puff of smoke, fragrant with the scent of apple wood, blew into the room.

Septimus was lying back in his chair, his eyes closed. He was concentrating on times. If he was right and the glow of fire he had seen had been on the pillar of rock, then the trout had been killed at about 7.30 p.m. on the previous night, Tuesday. The gull had been killed on Monday night – more accurately Tuesday morning – at about a quarter past three. So the two incidents had happened little more than sixteen hours apart. So someone had been extremely busy. As Mrs Beaton said, 'First catch your hare . . .'

A gull and a trout, and two fires, two miles apart, one on a tombstone, one on an inaccessible rock in the middle of a mountain stream. He did not know what was going on, but he was now quite certain that he was not dealing with a piece of mindless nonsense or casual hooliganism. Someone was working far too hard. It was . . . he selected words with care . . . it was planned, perverted and pretty sinister.

Sheep Shechem appeared to be crazy enough to do it, but what about the planning? Dylan Wesley Jones was violent enough – eggs at the Prince of Wales indeed! John Wesley Jones knew all there was to know about Hugh the wizard – and he had known that it was a fir that had been felled to make the bridge to the altar.

There was a crash of breaking glass, the curtains flew apart and something ricocheted off the chimney breast, hit Sandy's artificial leg with a hollow thump, and rolled into the centre of the hearth rug.

For perhaps a second Septimus sat entirely still, his mind registering facts. Sandy was O.K. – artificial legs had their advantages. It was not a bomb. It was a lump of slate wrapped in paper. The paper had come off the slate. It was a message, no doubt hostile. It could wait.

The glass had hardly ceased to tinkle to the floor as he hurled himself to his feet and ran for the kitchen door, knocking a chair over as he ran. He slammed the kitchen door behind him and stopped abruptly on the doorstep. It was quiet. There was no movement in the garden, no movement in the road. There was the tinny tinkling of the piano in the Maenofferen Arms. To his right the garden fell away to the lake, a high drystone wall at its bottom, at right angles to the lake shore. Catfoot, Septimus ran out of the gate, along the road and down the alley outside the wall, passing the boathouse at the bottom and so completing the square and coming back along the lake shore and up the side of the house under the shadow of the water-wheel. There was nothing and nobody. He went back through the kitchen and into the living-room.

'No luck,' he said. 'He must have shifted with the speed of light.'

'Someone doesn't love you,' replied the Colonel, holding out the sheet of paper. It was lined quarto, half a sheet torn from a loose-leaf folder. The message was in Welsh printed in block capitals with a green felt-tip.

'More or less, I think it says "Go home you English pig". Singular, not plural. You, old son, not me.' Septimus was thinking that 'pig' was the 'in' word among the disaffected for the police, and who in Hafod Maenen would use quarto loose-leaf paper? He could make a fair guess at the answer to that.

What he said was, 'What have I done to annoy Plaid Cymru?'

'You shouldn't come here investigating.' Sandy, despite his smashed window, was rather enjoying the little drama.

'I didn't.' Septimus was indignant. 'I came for a holiday. Anyway, I must go and see Wesley Jones. You be all right till I get back?'

Sandy grinned with a characteristic tightening of the jaw muscles which reminded Septimus of the past.

'I'll get the sten gun from the box room,' he said.

John Wesley Jones' cottage was up the alley opposite the

Maenofferen Arms. The hillside climbed so steeply that there were twelve steps up to the door, and the windows looked out on a panorama of mountains framed by the chimneys of the Royal Stores. Septimus looked a moment at the view in the deepening dusk. So much space, and so few people. He was aware of the remoteness and mystery of the high hills and of his own triviality, of their permanence and the transitoriness of his own life. For all the ravages of man, there was still an untouched quality about the high hills, an alien savagery. They had looked like that before man came. They had looked like that when the Welsh fought their desperate, doomed battle against the invading tribes from the east. They would still look like that when twentieth-century civilization was something to be pieced together painfully by archaeologists.

The door opened to his knock, and it was not John, but his son Dylan Wesley Jones, Septimus's bar-propping acquaintance of the previous evening.

Aware now of the relationship, Septimus could see the likeness between father and son. The boy's hair, though darker because untouched by age, was basically the same colour. There was the same bone structure to the face, the same brooding quality about the eyes.

'Good evening,' said Septimus, pleasantly enough. 'Your father's expecting me . . .'

He was cut off with a brief sentence in Welsh which sounded like a malediction. Septimus was irritated by the discourtesy.

'Look,' he said, trying to keep the friendly tone in his voice, 'you know English, and I don't know Welsh. I'm sorry about that, but I can't help it. We'd get on a lot better in English.'

'*Mae'n nhad allan.*'

Septimus kept a firm grip on his temper. After all the boy was only trying to irritate him.

'This is like a party game,' he said. 'Spot the Meaning. Is your father in?'

'*Yr ydwyf wedi dweud wrthych, ei fod allan.*'

'I give up,' said Septimus. 'You win the cut-glass fruit bowl. You'll have to tell me.'

Dylan leaned elaborately on the doorpost, folded his arms and gazed expressionlessly at the older man.

Septimus's imp of humour took charge of the situation. It was all so ludicrous. Deliberately mimicking Dylan, he leaned against the other doorpost and folded his arms, turning over in his mind dusty words from a long-disused vocabulary. Then he asked in pidgin Serbo-Croat, 'Can you direct me to the house of Madame Serbeyez? It is in the red-light district of the secret camp of Comrade Tito.'

He did not understand the reply because it was in Welsh. It sounded a little startled.

'It is of the utmost importance that I find her,' he went on seriously. 'She has my radio transmitter in her . . . in her . . .' What was the Serbo-Croat for attic? It did not matter. 'She has my radio transmitter in her gentlemen's convenience.'

This produced what appeared to be a mellifluous Welsh curse.

'But she is a parachutist, also a prostitute and needs the rope,' said Septimus plaintively.

Dylan's reply was cut off by the angry voice of his father speaking from the lane.

'Dylan! Stop your ill-mannered nonsense and show Mr Treloar into the house.'

Dylan said something abrupt, clattered down the steps, brushed past his father and disappeared round the corner.

John Wesley Jones was carrying a white enamel jug. He ushered Septimus into the cottage.

'Sorry about that, but that is my Dylan, I fear.'

'He'll get over it,' said Septimus.

'I suppose so. But I am sorry I was not here to greet you. I have been to the Maenofferen Arms for beer. You drink beer? Not like a Welsh Baptist of the strict variety. Good. And I hope Dylan was not too insulting. He can be terrible when he

45

has a mind. But then he is upset about the possibility that they will flood the valley. I cannot blame him for that. I am upset myself. To lose my home and move away. There's a miserable return for all the slate and coal and water and the ruined valleys, and holiday-makers in the summer thick as flies on a cow pat. No wonder Dylan does not like the English. But I am sorry he was rude for all that.'

5

John Wesley Jones

Septimus was sitting in a slat-backed wooden armchair on a rag rug by a coal fire in a black-leaded cooking range with two ovens and a battered copper kettle hissing on the hob. Wesley Jones busied himself with tankards while the priest gazed round with interest. The cottage, he guessed, was much as a slate miner's cottage must have been in 1900. The steep stairs went straight up out of the living-room. The floor was slabbed slate. There was a big Welsh dresser taking up the whole of one wall. It would have raised a fortune in a London sale-room.

A brass oil lamp stood in the middle of the scrubbed table. It cast a warm glow on slate and brass and black-leaded iron. Satisfactorily there were pottery dogs on the dresser – a positive stud of them, and texts on the wall. 'Thou God Seest Me.' 'Vengeance is Mine. I will Repay Saith the Lord.' The only unexpected feature was that the alcoves on either side of the fireplace were full from slate floor to plank ceiling with books. From the flowered and hideous wallpaper to the brass-bound family Bible in the middle of the dresser, the room might have remained unchanged for half a century.

'Now Mr Treloar, what can I do for you?' Wesley Jones put a pewter tankard by Septimus's elbow. Septimus took it and drank deeply before replying.

'Hugh-ap-Lloyd,' he said.

Wesley Jones smiled into the fire as if he shared with it some secret joke. 'Ah! That would be on account of the dead bird the Colonel found on his tombstone?'

'You know about that then?' Uninvited, Septimus was pouring himself more beer. He saw Wesley Jones' eyebrows go up a fraction. But he did not care. He had his reasons.

'All Hafod Maenen knows. Only some say it was a sheep and some a dead baby that he found.' In his turn Septimus looked surprised.

'Mr Treloar. You are an Englishman and perhaps do not understand the ways of a Welsh village tiny as this. If I go out the back at seven in the morning instead of eight – which is my usual time more or less, Myfanwy Nextdoor will notice out of her scullery window, and she will tell May Parry when she goes to the shop, and May will tell someone else. So when in the evening I go to the Maenofferen to wash the dust from my throat, Evan Pritchard will say, "Oh, John Wesley Jones, man! They told me the ambulance had taken you to Blaenau Ffestiniog for a stoppage of the bowels." ' He was laughing and Septimus laughed with him. 'Yes,' he said. 'My village is just like that.'

'Now Hugh-ap-Lloyd,' said Wesley Jones, 'he was a saint supposedly – so some of the books say. And some of them say he was a wizard. Caradoc Lloyd, who knows more about it than most, says that he was the original of King Arthur's magician, Merlin.'

Septimus put down his tankard. 'What? In 1732?'

'Oh, the date on the stone! Man! That's not a tombstone. Just a memorial they put up to him. The minister at the time wanted to put it in the church – he was a bit of a wizard

47

himself by all accounts. Only the deacons would not have it, being godly men. No, the stories of Hugh-ap-Lloyd are older than that. Much older. A thousand years and more. Now, if you had gone to the top of the altar instead of just to where Sheep Shechem had been fishing, you would have seen the best evidence for yourself.' He paused, so that Septimus wondered if he was doing a bit of fishing on his own behalf. He said nothing and the Welshman continued.

'At the top you would have found a real altar, squared with chisels. And there is a carved border which Caradoc Lloyd says is merlins and holly and mistletoe. The scholars say it goes back to the dark times before Christianity came to Cymru.'

'And what do you think?' Septimus asked. Wesley Jones stooped and poked the fire. 'I do not know. I have been there once. Many years ago. It is a terrible place. But to me the border was just marks on the stone.' He got up to trim the lamp.

'And what of Hugh-ap-Lloyd?' Septimus asked.

'Have you ever heard of the Red Book of Ifan Ddu? But of course you have not. The Red Book is old, very old. It has been in Caradoc Lloyd's family since no one knows when, and Caradoc Lloyd is descended from Hugh-ap-Lloyd supposedly. Ifan Ddu . . .' He paused gazing into the fire as if he could see Ifan Ddu's face there. Septimus was aware of the grandfather clock ticking solemnly in the corner, measured, like a heartbeat. '. . . Ifan Ddu was a great Welsh hero who defended Cymru from the invaders.'

'Tried to keep the English out,' said Septimus.

Wesley Jones smiled, and the firelight flickered across the stern lines of his face. 'Man! We are not talking about tourists. What is English? What is British if you go back as I have done? Some say the Red Book talks of the last stand of the Roman British against the tribes from over the sea, when the legions had gone and civilization was crumbling.' He paused again. Septimus, quite out of his historical depth, said nothing.

'Some say Ifan Ddu was the true King Arthur just as Hugh-ap-Lloyd was Merlin. But you will have to ask Caradoc Lloyd about that.' He reached for the enamel jug and laughed. 'Man! You have finished all the beer! And you a minister.'

'I'm terribly sorry,' said Septimus contritely. 'How greedy of me. But I was rather thirsty. Sandy's curry . . .' He left the question of Sandy's curry in the air since they had in fact dined on beef. 'Do let me go and get some more.' He stood up, reaching for the jug. Wesley Jones moved it out of his reach.

'I would not think of it. You are my guest. I will get some more. It will not take a moment.' He closed the door softly as he went out of the cottage.

Septimus winked at one of the china dogs on the dresser. He burped impolitely. 'Excuse me,' he said to the china dog, 'but I had to get master out of the house for a minute.' The china dog took no manner of notice of this confession. Septimus waited until he heard the gate click, then he got up and walked softly up the stairs. Had the china dog been given to thought, it would have been surprised by the speed and silence of so big a man.

There were two bedrooms, one on either side of the microscopic landing. That to the left was neat, bare, like a prison cell. It had a narrow iron bedstead, an oak chest of drawers, and one corner was curtained for use as a wardrobe. The other bedroom was chaotic. An unmade bed, a table under the window covered with books and files. There were books and clothes in piles on the floor, used cups on every available flat surface, and the walls were covered with a hotch-potch of posters: Che Guevara, a scantily clad young lady draped across the controls of an airliner, romantic illustrations from *The Lord of the Rings*, and urgent invocations in Welsh and in lurid colour which Septimus could not translate but which he guessed he would disapprove of if he could. He smiled wryly. It all made him feel so very old. He turned over the books on

49

the table. Sociology and Economics and Industrial History. Evidently Dylan, despite the rustication for the plot against the Prince of Wales, was still doing some work. *The Industrial Revolution and Eighteenth-Century Wales* published by the University of Wales and printed in English was held open at page 102 with a green felt-tip pen. Septimus smiled. It had not really been a very difficult guess when you considered how small the community was and who might conceivably be given to hurling rocks about the place. He tore a sheet from one of the loose-leaf folders, wrote a short message on it in block letters with the felt-tip, folded the paper and put it in his pocket, and then put everything on the desk exactly as he had found it.

When Wesley Jones returned he was standing by the bookcase in the living-room turning over the pages of George Borrow's *Wild Wales*.

'Looking at the Red Book are you?' The Welshman closed the door behind him.

'You've got a copy then?'

'Only extracts, man. The whole thing's never been published. If you really want to see the Red Book you'll have to go to the Plas and ask Caradoc Lloyd.'

'I'll do that,' said Septimus.

Wesley Jones put the beer on the table and took a book from the shelf. They settled themselves in front of the fire, and the Welshman opened the book, tilting it as he turned the leaves to catch the light of the lamp.

'It is very difficult, the Welsh. It is so old, and there is a lot I do not understand. But it says that invaders came from where the sun rises over the mountains. And it says that Ifan Ddu opposed them, but he did not . . . prevail. And that he made a last stand in the Pass of the Mists above the Lake of the Pigs.' Septimus, who was leaning back with his tankard clasped on his stomach, opened his eyes. 'Lake of the Pigs? Llyn-y-Moch?'

'So the scholars say.'

'And the Pass of the Mists?'

'Nobody knows really, but Caradoc Lloyd thinks that it is the pass from this cwm into Cwm Barlwyd, which is where he lives.'

Septimus remembered the pass. He had come through it before the mist clamped down and he had got lost.

Wesley Jones continued with his halting translation of the Welsh. 'Ifan Ddu spoke to Hugh-ap-Lloyd, "By Christ and by Mary, here I stand. Let them do what they will!" And the Druid answered, "Then you shall be swept into the sea." "What will be, will be," said the king, and he had been Pilate.

'But the wizard said, "Not so. For this Christ and this Mary are weak. And I called on the old gods of stream and wood, of lake and mountain, you should see other manner of happening." And Ifan Ddu said, "Let it be so."

'Hugh-ap-Lloyd took the white bird to the defiled grove by the edge of the lake and offered it with the sword of the new faith. And the wind whispered, and the stream roared, and the lake murmured. But the gods did not reply.

'Then the wizard took the silver fish from the running stream and carried it to the altar of running water and offered it with the sword of the new faith. And the wind roared over the llyn, and the invaders murmured, for they heard the old gods speak. But yet they did not awake.'

Wesley Jones put the book down for a moment and poured more beer. 'That first bit was what the Colonel found, Mr Treloar. Pity you did not go to the top of the altar to see if anyone had fulfilled the second part of the story.' He stared at Septimus over the rim of his tankard, but Septimus refused to be drawn. It all fitted, he thought. It fitted a damn sight too neatly. 'Go on,' he said.

'Then Hugh-ap-Lloyd took the black lamb of the white ewe and offered it . . .' He hesitated in his translating. 'Here it begins to defeat me . . . with the sword of the new faith on the . . . it's probably "hearthstone of the lord's fortress", or it might be "king's castle". And the wind shouted in his strength, and the torrent tumbled the rock, and the lake rose as if it had been the sea, and the invader was tormented by the power of the old gods.' He stopped translating. 'And that's as far as I can get. The rest is too difficult for me. Hugh-ap-Lloyd did something else, because you get the phrase about the sword of the new faith again, only it's twisted round so it might mean the new sword of the old faith. But what he did is too much of a mixture of nonsense Welsh and corrupt Latin for the likes of me.'

Septimus sat up and started to put on his innocent country parson act.

'So that's it,' he said. 'Thank you very much, John, for a most instructive evening. And thank you for the beer.'

'What do you make of it, Mr Treloar?'

Septimus was already half way to the door. 'Make of it? I haven't any idea. Someone seems to be behaving very wickedly and foolishly, and I just want to turn it all over in my mind. So thank you for all your help, and I know you'll excuse me running away like this. Oh! and one thing, John. It would be the most enormous help if you could write out that translation for me. The most enormous help. You will do that, won't you? Thank you so very much, so very much indeed. Good! That's splendid. Goodnight my dear man, goodnight!' He closed the door gently behind him and went quickly down the steps.

'Well!' said Wesley Jones in considerable astonishment. 'And the Welsh are supposed to be able to talk themselves out of things.'

Half an hour later Septimus was sitting on the low wall surrounding the Mill wheel. He had sat there on his way back from Wesley Jones' cottage because it was a convenient place to sit, and because he had entirely forgotten where he was going. To his right the ridge of the boathouse roof was stark against the phosphorescence of the lake. The clouds were low over the mountains so that he could not see their outline against the night sky. He sat, playing with his pipe which he had filled but not lighted. The case – if there was a case – was making some sort of progress. A trout and a white bird. So two of the events from the Red Book had been copied.

Logically a black sheep should follow. Then perhaps something else which Wesley Jones could not – or would not – translate. What was it all supposed to achieve? By the way the 'old gods' seemed to be getting up steam he would hazard a guess that in the end they did for the English invader. Certainly there was plenty of bitterness in the valley about the 'English invader' in the twentieth century. He remembered the unreasoning hostility of Evan Pritchard, the landlord of the Maenofferen Arms. There was Dylan. Dylan had thrown a rock through Sandy's window to scare off the English 'pig'. That implied a bitterness of no mean order. He remembered Sandy telling him of Gwillym Parry's hand crushing the packet of tobacco as he talked of the plan to dam the lake and turn the lovely valley into a reservoir. There was certainly plenty of bitterness, and plenty of good reason for bitterness. He set himself to try and imagine what he would do if a series of bland officials with the law on their side stole his home, and pulled it down and drowned the graves of his ancestors. He remembered the family Bible on the dresser in the Wesley Jones parlour. He could imagine the entries, Gwillyms and Myfanwys and Beths and Dylans, the painstaking handwriting and the ink brown with age. And it would all be destroyed to provide electricity for the TV sets of an alien who thought of Wales as a place of toy railways and dark-haired women in pointed hats and shawls. Yes. He could imagine himself putting bombs under pipelines, throwing surveying equipment into a lake, even – like Dylan – making juvenile insults and throwing rocks through windows. But animal sacrifice? Trying to make an old wives' tale come true? No. Not an old wives' tale. One of the sagas of a great and honourable people. But even so? Macbeth was a great

53

play, but what about someone who played the three witches for real? You would certainly have to be mad to believe that it could be made to work in the twentieth century. Mad with a special kind of madness – which might well not show on the surface. And then, was it madness? He knew a fair amount about the powers of witch-doctors and the like. He had once been sent to Trinidad to help with an investigation into a particularly revolting ritual murder. Who was he to pontificate about what was possible in these high hills with their buried past, their memories of Druids and golden groves and the power of the wizard? He took his unlit pipe from his mouth and said softly, 'Dammit, Septimus, stick to facts.' He had a few. Dylan, for instance, was a violent and unbalanced young man, and his father might well know more than he pretended to know.

And, of course, Sheep Shechem – always Sheep Shechem. But could such a 'natural' be expected to know the contents of the Red Book? And if he did, could even a natural believe that animal sacrifice was going to stop the Electricity Board. A dam on one side – all the complications of engineers and scientific tests, of theodolites and bulldozers – and on the other a wild Celtic myth about gulls and fish. It was improbable to the point of being ludicrous. And yet . . . and yet . . . in these bewitched mountains anything might be possible.

A wind came out of the hills. It ruffled the surface of the lake. It was followed by a stronger gust, and then a flurry of rain. Septimus got up and tapped out his pipe, entirely unconscious of the fact that he had never lighted the contents of the bowl. He made for the kitchen door as the surface of the lake began to dance with the rain. 'And the lake rose like the sea,' he thought. As the rain reached him he ran.

Septimus woke to the howling and growling of the wind. The thick stone walls of the Mill paid no regard to the wildness of the storm. It was, after all, what they had been built to withstand. The masons who had erected it in the eighteenth century had no illusions about Welsh weather. It was, even so, a night in which you could believe anything: legends about Merlin, the efficacy of animal sacrifice, stories out of the Red Book and the *Arabian Nights*. He thought of Ifan Ddu, of Hugh-ap-Lloyd, of John and Dylan Wesley Jones, of Gwillym Parry. He tried to imagine himself as a young Welshman passionately in love with his beautiful country. Yes. He could understand the anger, the passion about the language, the defacing of traffic signs, the occupation of holiday cottages. But to try to use magic? It did not seem so impossible with the storm throbbing around the Mill, but he recognized that he was only churning over the ground he had covered earlier, and that was valueless, so he switched off speculation and lay listening to the storm. He was wrong when he said that it did not affect the thick walls of the Mill. There would be a lull, then a slam of wind like a physical blow which would rattle the windows and the room would seem to brace itself against the powers of the forces outside. He supposed it was something to do with the sudden change in pressure. Or perhaps it was to do with the 'old gods'? He grinned in the darkness. If he stayed long enough in the Principality he would be sacrificing maidens himself. He rolled over and switched on the light. It was half past two. Turning on the light made the sound of the storm seem more remote, as if electricity could hold back the elements.

A picture came into his mind. Steel pylons groaning in the storm, trembling in the wind as they strode like aliens from another planet across the gale-wracked mountainside, the cables in their catenary curves blowing sideways as they took the strain of the wind. Carrying power for electric tooth-brushes and blankets, for refrigerators and television sets — and for more important things — factories and kidney machines and cookers for housewives feeding their menfolk. But the pylons and cables were the invaders. The hills belonged to the wind and the rain. They had been there before the coming of man. A sudden thought crossed Septimus's mind as he lay speculating, listening to the storm. It would take a veritable Queen's Scout among wizards to light a fire for sacrificing a black lamb on such a night. It was a comforting thought since it gave him more time.

He was about to turn off the bedside light when he remembered the Biblical reference on Hugh-ap-Lloyd's memorial stone. He made a guess about the meaning of 'Cyntaf' and tried 1 *Samuel*, chapter 28, verse 13. It came from the account of King Saul's visit to the Witch of Endor on the eve of the battle of Gilboa in which Saul met his death.

'And the king said unto her, be not afraid: for what sawest thou? And the woman said unto Saul, I saw gods ascending out of the earth.'

6

Trouble with Surveyors

'Anything can happen in Wales, Mr Treloar, but all the same it's hard to know what to make of it.' It was the following rain-washed morning. Septimus was talking to Gwillym Parry in the shop where he had gone to buy tobacco for Sandy. May was busy making up an order, and Gwyn was sitting in one corner, building a castle of baked-bean tins.

'Louts is it? Coming into the valley from Blaenau Ffestiniog perhaps, playing silly games in the old chapel.'

'But how would they get here?' asked Septimus.

'There are the tunnels under the mountain. You can walk through from Cwm Barlwyd — if you know what you are doing, that is.'

'Is it safe?'

'Safe? Nothing in slate mining is safe, not really. Tunnelling like worms into the heart of a mountain. They're riddled, man. Down and down, level below level until you are a hundred feet below the sea itself and it takes a day to bring a block to the light. And mile after mile of tunnels and chambers and galleries. And when the slate has been taken and the pumps are turned off . . . the water comes back.' He moved across to the post office part of the shop. 'But yes, it is safe to walk through – if you know which tunnels to use.'

'But . . .' began Septimus. He broke off as the bell on the door jangled and Dylan Wesley Jones came into the shop. He saw Septimus and quickly went out again. 'Excuse me,' said Septimus, making for the door.

'Man! You've forgotten Sandy's tobacco.' But the door had already slammed behind Septimus.

'Oy! Dylan. I want a word with you.' Septimus shouted at Dylan's receding back, but the youth continued to walk rapidly away. He did not even turn. In this he was unwise, but it did not occur to him that an elderly clergyman might be so undignified as to chase him. But for his age and size Septimus ran fast – and quietly, and he never gave a moment's thought to his dignity. So that by the time Dylan realized what was happening, it was far too late. A hand big as a frying-pan descended on his shoulder, and he was spun round with his arm twisted expertly behind his back. He swore in Welsh, and then because of the pain in his shoulder, 'Let go, you great gorilla! You're hurting me.'

'And what's the Welsh for that, my lad? Or would you prefer it in pidgin Serbo-Croat?' Septimus's face was grim as he fumbled with his disengaged hand in his jacket pocket. He produced two pieces of paper and fanned them out clumsily between finger and thumb. One was the message which had been hurled through the Mill window, the other was the piece he had taken from Dylan's bedroom.

'What about these, then?' He thrust the pieces of paper

57

close to Dylan's face so that he could read what Septimus had written. 'Dylan Wesley Jones heaved a rock through the Colonel's window.'

'What about it, then?' said Septimus, tightening his grip.

'Ouch!' said the boy, and then, 'All right, I did it. It's a fair cop. Isn't that what I'm supposed to say to pigs?'

Septimus let go of his arm so suddenly that Dylan spun in a half-circle. Septimus sat down on the low wall of a cottage garden and took out his pipe. 'Why don't you grow up?' he asked. Dylan was rubbing his shoulder and did not reply.

'As to what you say to pigs – that's your business. After all you live in the Valley of Pigs, if I've got the Welsh right. As to heaving rocks through Sandy's window, there's several things to say . . .'

His voice rose suddenly into a sharp tone of command. 'No. Don't go away,' then more loudly still, 'I shan't chase you again. I shall have you arrested.' Dylan came reluctantly back.

'Come and sit down, boy, and let's talk.' Dylan subsided on to the wall and Septimus looked sidelong at him, a smile on his battered face.

'I'm an English bastard,' he said. 'I live in East Anglia, and I'm so ignorant, I don't even know whether it's Welsh water that comes out of the tap. One of my churchwardens owns a caravan in Criccieth, and for all I know he's got a string of brothels in Portmadoc.' Septimus noted the twitch of Dylan's lips, and so continued in the same vein. 'Actually, I'm an absentee landlord myself. I've got a converted Primitive Methodist Chapel in Bethesda, and I hold all the services in English, and you can only come to them if you're a tourist from the Midlands and are wearing a top hat, spats and pin-stripe trousers.' He offered Dylan his tobacco pouch. 'You don't smoke? Sensible of you. Filthy habit. Seriously, Dylan, I'm just an old Anglican parson and ex-copper that can't sing "Bread of Heaven" in Welsh and believes in bishops – don't laugh. If you saw my bishop you wouldn't find him funny. And you're a Welsh student – so why can't we be friends?'

'All right,' said Dylan, smiling, accepting Septimus as a person for the first time.

'I don't suppose that pub's open yet,' said Septimus. Dylan replied with a flash of his old spirit. 'Not for you, it won't be.'

Septimus went across the road. Evan Pritchard was sweeping the bar in desultory fashion. 'Morning, squire,' he said, rubbing his unshaven chin speculatively.

'Good morning. I don't suppose you're open yet?'

'Well, as to that . . . there's the Law. But Dai Truncheon only comes up the valley twice a week, and today ain't his day. So what'll you have?'

Septimus ordered two pints of bitter. 'Going to drink it outside, are you?' asked Evan as he drew the beer. 'With young Dylan? Well, if you see Dai coming up the road on his bicycle come inside. Dai don't go looking for trouble, but I wouldn't want to give him a heart attack. Your health, squire.' He paused and was suddenly conspiratorial. 'See you twisting young Dylan's arm. Sacrificing seagulls on tombstones. Could have been Dylan. He's crazy enough. Do anything to stop the English turning the valley into a reservoir.'

Septimus noted that the landlord apparently knew the story from the Red Book. But then everyone in Hafod Maenen seemed to know everything anyway. 'Wouldn't you want to stop them?' he asked.

The landlord shrugged. 'Do what they like for me. So long as they give me decent compensation.'

Dylan had moved across to the bench outside the Maenofferen Arms. Septimus put the tankards on the table and sat down.

'Now, Dylan,' he said, 'before we do anything else, let's dispose of this rock-heaving. One. Colonel Sanderson is an old friend of mine and I won't have people busting his windows. Two. You could kill someone with a hunk of slate like that. Suppose little Gwyn Parry had been in the room?' He stopped, unaware of the sternness of his expression.

'The child could not have been there,' said Dylan defensively. 'It was too late in the evening.'

'How do you know? Sandy might have invited him to dinner. Then there's three. I could throw the book at you. Anything from "loitering with intent" to "attempted murder". But I won't—provided you come off it. Here's your pieces of paper, and don't do it again, the next English cop might be more dyspeptic than I am.'

Dylan put the pieces of paper in his pocket. 'Thank you, Mr Treloar. I am sorry I was so unpleasant. It is just that I cannot bear seeing what is happening to my country. My father has already lost one home to the reservoirs. Llyn Celyn they call it. There is a drowned village there. Capelcelyn it was called. There is a little chapel on the new road that they have built.'

'Yes, I remember it,' said Septimus.

'My mother is remembered there,' said Dylan bitterly. 'She died, you see, when she knew that she was to be turned out and her home flooded, and nothing could stop them. And . . .' He paused and Septimus caught the glint of tears in his eyes. 'And what?' he asked gently.

'And . . . and so it is not surprising that I feel strongly about this valley and my father being turned out for a second time.' Septimus noted that it was not what he had been going to say, but judged it best to change the subject.

'I'm sorry about that,' he said sincerely, 'but I'm not letting you off over the rock-heaving just because I'm a soft-hearted old ruin. I really need your help.'

'My help?' Dylan's astonishment was very obvious.

'Yes. Your father thinks I ought to have a word with Sheep Shechem, and I need an interpreter.'

Dylan laughed. 'Sheep Shechem! You will certainly need an interpreter with him. He is—what do you call it in English?—a natural. He lives over the mountain in one of

60

Caradoc Lloyd's cottages with his old mother. He knows no English . . . at least . . .' he laughed again, selfconsciously this time, '. . . at least he pretends to know no English.'

'This afternoon?' said Septimus. Dylan agreed. 'But it will do you no good,' he said.

'Why?' Septimus asked.

'Sheep Shechem hates the English, that is why.'

'Why the English?' Septimus asked.

'Well, not just the English. All strangers. You know that he nearly killed a man from the Council?' Septimus nodded.

'Well, he was an Englishman. The authorities, they have tried to turn him out so many times. Some of the stories are very funny, man – and some not funny at all. But he hates all foreigners. They will do him harm, and his mother, and the valleys that he loves and the animals. The only person he really trusts is Caradoc Lloyd who owns the cottage they live in. If you are going to talk to Sheep Shechem, you will need a real Welshman to keep you from harm.'

'Charming,' said Septimus, and then, 'Glad to know I shall have one.' They parted and Septimus returned to the Mill well satisfied with his morning's work. There were several things he hoped to learn from Dylan, apart from needing him as an interpreter.

In the kitchen May Parry was busy at the cooker.

'Hullo, May,' he said in surprise. 'How did you get here?' She smiled.

'You were too busy with Dylan to see me. I saw you, though. Drinking out of hours. I'm surprised at you, and you a minister.'

Septimus changed the subject. 'Where's my friend Gwyn?'

'He has gone round to the quarry with Uncle John – John Wesley Jones, that is. Not really his uncle, of course. But that is what Gwyn calls him.'

Septimus paused, his hand on the living-room door.

'May. Dylan's just been telling me about how they used to live at Capelcelyn.' The smile faded from May's kindly face, and she stood a moment, floury hands resting on the kitchen table.

'His mother and the little girl. It was a terrible thing, and not surprising that John Wesley Jones had the breakdown and spent all those months in the hospital.' Septimus came back into the centre of the kitchen. 'Tell me, May,' he said.

She sat down at the table and told him with an un-English fluency and the eye for detail of the born story-teller.

As Dylan had said, his mother, already sick, had given up all desire to live when it was certain that the village was doomed.

'Lived there for generations, they had. Her father was a farmer, and his father before him. John Wesley Jones has the family Bible with all the names in it, going right back. Took to her bed, and would neither eat nor drink, so they say. Turned her face to the wall and died.' The girl had been called Ronwen. Three years younger than Dylan, she had been left at school in Bala, living with an aunt and coming home to Hafod Maenen at the weekends. Wednesday was a half-holiday, and the child used to go off — so the aunt thought — playing with her friends. In fact, she quite often took the Portmadoc bus and got off at the chapel. 'Took flowers for her mother,' said May.

There had come one Wednesday in early spring when she had not returned to the aunts. They had found her next morning. Evidently she had walked out along the dam and slipped into the water. 'It was an accident, of course,' said May. 'She was a happy child — when she was not grieving for her mam and for the house under the water. But there she was, and the flowers she had gathered floating in the water beside her. John Wesley Jones went mad. Attacked a Water Board man in a shop in Portmadoc. There was a court case. But they were kind to him on account of what had happened. But he spent months in the hospital.'

Septimus walked slowly into the living-room. He was thinking of a picture he had once seen — pre-Raphaelite was it? – of the drowned Ophelia. But it was Ophelia who had gone mad, not Hamlet. He had died righting the wrong that had been done to his father.

Sandy was sitting by the fire reading *The Times*, his spectacles low on his nose so that he looked like Mr Pickwick.

'You've been a long time,' he said. 'Did you get my tobacco?'

'Dammit!' said Septimus. 'I left it in the shop.'

Sandy beamed over his spectacles. 'I know you did. May brought it.'

Septimus aimed an inaccurate slash at a thistle with Sandy's second-best walking-stick. 'Gwillym Parry says it was tearaways coming through the slate tunnels from Blaenau Ffestiniog,' he said.

'They'd have to know the mines, wouldn't they?' Dylan replied.

They were striding side by side along the lane towards the bottom of the lake, sheep scattering before them. Septimus pointed with the stick.

'If you're going to light a fire in the quarry, you come from the village, or through the village, or through the tunnels, or over the top.'

'Take a long time over the top,' said Dylan.

'Who would know the way through?'

'Sheep Shechem for one,' replied Dylan, 'but I wouldn't choose him if I wanted guiding. My father – since he's your chief suspect. Any old quarryman who worked there. But I don't think it's layabouts. Too lazy and too stupid. Get lost in the tunnels.'

'What do you think?'

Dylan shrugged with a Celtic comprehensiveness.

'Someone fulfilling the legend from the Red Book?' suggested Septimus.

'The fish and the bird and the lamb? It would seem so.'

Septimus said nothing. So Dylan did know the Red Book.

63

The young man went on as if he had read Septimus's thoughts. 'Oh, yes. I know the Red Book. You couldn't be the son of my father and not know it.' He turned to Septimus and grinned. 'I'd do it too, if I thought it would get rid of the Electricity Board.'

They reached the end of the valley and turned across the bottom of the lake. To their right, the country fell away to the estuary and they had a wide view of cloud-shadowed blues and greens and the bright yellow of sand. Septimus was reminded of stout Cortes gazing with eagle eyes at the Pacific. He could not remember the poet, and anyway he was looking at the Irish Sea.

A little above the path stood the wooden hut belonging to the engineers who were investigating the possibilities of the dam. It looked ugly and out of place among the rocks and heather. Above it, on an outcrop was a short, dark man in a fawn duffle coat. He was folding the tripod legs of a theodolite. Dylan called something in Welsh. It did not sound very friendly. The engineer took no notice. He shouldered his theodolite and came down to the path. Dylan repeated his remark and was once again ignored. Septimus, tempted to strangle Dylan there and then, grinned his friendliest country parson grin at the engineer. 'Afternoon,' he said. 'Not too bad weather for your job.'

The engineer ceased to look quite so sour. 'Afternoon,' he said. 'Not so bad. Nearly finished now.' Septimus identified the accent as West Midlands.

'Are they going to turn it into a reservoir?' he asked.

'Couldn't say,' the other man replied. 'I only do the surveying. The bosses, they decide.'

There was a torrent of angry Welsh from Dylan, and to Septimus's astonishment the engineer turned on him and replied with an equally angry, equally fluent flood of Welsh.

They stood facing one another, trying to shout one another down, Dylan gesticulating like a stage Frenchman, the engineer gripping his theodolite as if he was about to use it as a medieval mace. They were like a couple of sheepdogs disputing the ownership of a tup. By the time Septimus had recovered from his surprise the confrontation had come close to blows. He grabbed Dylan and dragged him away by main force.

Like embattled ships of the line parted by the wind, they continued to hurl abuse at one another until Septimus had hauled Dylan round the shoulder of rock and out of sight.

Dylan was white of face and trembling with passion, and Septimus was startled by the vitriolic power of his rage. He remembered May Parry's story about the family background. He released his hold and said evenly, 'You do get excited. Do yourself a mischief one of these days.' Dylan relaxed and smiled. The change was startling in its swiftness. 'Bah!' he said. 'Traitor. A renegade Welshman. Doing the dirty work for the vandals. But what can you expect from a southerner?'

7

Sheep Shechem

They were climbing now, away from the lake along a boggy and scarcely perceptible track until the scant sheep-grazing gave place to gaunt scree and the path became a fearsome zig-zag, a mere flattening scarcely six inches wide on the surface of the countless millions of flakes of rock which time and weather had chiselled from the towering cliffs. Septimus looked up at the pinnacles and slabs of Craig-y-Moch, marvelling that once, when he was young, he would have wished to pit his climbing skill against those unforgiving faces, that once he could have climbed them. Soon he had no time for speculation. Dylan, intent on proving something or other, was setting a cracking pace and was already nearly fifty yards ahead.

'Right, my lad!' Septimus thought. 'I can give you thirty years, but I'll still give you a run for your money.' He lengthened his stride, sending the stones clattering down the scree. The distance between them began to close.

Up they went, across and across the forty-five degree slope of the unstable scree like two tiny insects beneath the blind rock giants of the crags, the stones beneath their feet sliding and clattering, echoing from the cliffs like lonely voices. Once Septimus looked back, and the lake was already a mere pool below them, and on the shore the houses of Hafod Maenen looked like a toy village made from a few match-boxes. Beyond and above, stretching to the limit of sight, there were hills and the glint of lakes rising one beyond another to the cloud-capped summit of Snowdon.

Once his stick jammed in a crevice and he nearly fell. He recovered and stumbled on, his heart pounding, the salt sweat running across his brow and into his eyes. 'I will not stop,' he thought as the blood thundered in his temples, 'I will not look up. I will not cry halt. I will go on until I drop.' He knew it was foolish, but there was a mulish strain about him which had surprised many people in the past and had saved his life on two occasions. Then came the shaft of self-mockery – 'You'll go on until you have a coronary, you silly old fool.'

Suddenly it was over. He stumbled up yet another length of the horrible path, around a rock, and there was no more scree, only grass and Dylan lying full length on it. He was on his back, and, as far as the heaving of his lungs allowed, he was laughing.

'I expected to leave you much farther behind,' he panted.

Septimus was incapable of speech. He pitched on to the grass and lay full length, gasping. It was five minutes before

66

he felt strong enough to sit up. When he managed it, Dylan was propped against the rock gazing over Snowdonia.

He smiled at Septimus. 'Look,' he said, 'there's Cymru. That's what I care about.' He started to point. 'There is Cnicht – they call it the Welsh Matterhorn, but I think it is more beautiful. And that is Tryfan. Did you know there are wild goats on Tryfan? And beyond . . . those are the Glyders. And that is the Snowdon Horseshoe . . . and there is Yr Aran . . . and there is Snowdon herself, Yr Wyddfa.' He paused a moment and then went on more softly, not really speaking to Septimus at all. 'The place of the eagles. The highest mountain in Wales. Raped, like an old whore, by ten million tourists. And a snack bar on the top, just like Cardiff railway station. Do you wonder I am bitter, Mr Treloar?' Septimus was gazing into the blue distance. He replied very softly, without turning to Dylan.

'My home's Cornwall. My father was a soldier. He inherited the family estate. We had our own beach and our own boat when we were kids. It was all a long time ago.' His face was sad, remembering. 'They've turned the house into a motel, there's a caravan park above the beach, and a public loo where we used to moor our boat.'

He stood up and thumped Dylan across the shoulder. 'So come out of the Celtic twilight, Dylan, and let's get on. Remember, I'm a Celt with the best of you.'

They set off up the grassy slope above the cliffs, moving diagonally towards the ravine of the Afon Maenen. High in the saddle of the mountains they came to a derelict quarry with the usual chaos of ruined buildings and crazy tips of slate waste. They panted up to the skyline by two precipitous inclines, until at last they stood beneath the rotting drum of the winch-house at the very top.

They crossed the boggy watershed between the two valleys, and came down by more precipitous inclines to another derelict quarry at the head of another lake. The quarry was like all the others, a sad and lonely place, except that at one

67

end of an otherwise derelict row of cottages there was a slated roof, windows with glass in them, and a chimney with smoke coming out of it. Dylan pointed. 'That's where Sheep Shechem lives.' He saw the look of surprise on Septimus's face and laughed as they moved down over the clinking slate. 'You are thinking, "Why do the Council allow it?" but you do not know Welsh Councils, nor do you know Sheep Shechem or his mother. The Council send notices to quit, numberless as autumn leaves, and he uses them to light his cigarettes. He says he cannot read.'

Septimus smiled. He was beginning to appreciate the healthy Welsh attitude to the workings of bureaucracy. After all, if your country had been occupied by what was in effect a foreign power for half a millennium, you were likely to develop a peculiar, not to say cavalier, attitude to the rules of your conqueror.

They came to the occupied cottage. Beside it there were several small enclosures running down to the lake. They were fenced with slabs of slate thrust into the ground, rusty wire and brambles twined between them. One enclosure contained a sow and half a dozen piglets, another about ten lambs, and a third a very small and very muddy donkey. There were bedraggled hens everywhere, and a convoy of ducks paddling in the mud where the mountain stream lost itself in the reeds. The little yard outside the cottage was cluttered like a junk stall in an open-air market. There was a mangle of vast antiquity with the biggest wooden rollers Septimus had ever seen. There was a pile of rotting timber beside a crazy sawing horse. In one corner was an empty pigsty, and in another a beautiful dovecote built of dressed slate and complete with doves. There were the decaying remains of a very ancient motor cycle. Septimus's observant eye noted that it had last been taxed in 1940. Propped beneath the one, heavily curtained window of the little cottage was a woman's bicycle. It was of the old 'sit-up-and-beg' variety, complete with string guard to protect voluminous skirts from the back wheel, and a basket big enough for a week's washing attached by wire to the rusty handlebars. It was battered and muddy, but clearly a going concern. Septimus approved of it wholeheartedly. It was the sort of machine Queen Victoria might have ridden had Prince Albert permitted her to bicycle.

Dylan knocked at the battered door of the cottage. Nothing happened, except that the heavy curtains at the window twitched and Septimus pretended not to see the white face which peeped out at them.

Dylan knocked again and the curtain dropped back into place. There was a gentle cooing of doves, the cluck of hens, the noises of lambs and piglets, and the chuckle of water. Then the door opened three inches and a face peeped out of the crack, the thin face of a very old woman. She spoke sharply in Welsh, her voice hostile. Dylan replied, and after a short exchange the door closed and was bolted.

Dylan turned to Septimus. 'She says that Shechem is away up the mountain seeking sheep for Pandy Harris. She does not know when he will be back—perhaps tomorrow morning. But we can wait for him if we want to.' The only thing to be said about Dylan's expression was that he was obviously not smiling.

'Well,' said Septimus, 'I haven't come all this way just to go away again, so let's make ourselves comfortable.' They went and sat by the stream, their backs against rock, watching the fingerling trout dash in panic from their shadows.

'You never told me about Sheep Shechem's mother,' Septimus said.

'You never asked me.'

'Well, as we've got to wait for the gentleman, you might as well tell me now.'

'Shechem's father was a quarryman,' said Dylan, 'and he worked in this quarry when it was working and the three of them lived in this cottage. Shechem was always a bit simple, seemingly—no harm in him really, except when he gets angry. He's so strong, you see. Anyway, the old man died, but Caradoc Lloyd, who is the owner, let Shechem and his mother stay on in the cottage, and Shechem made himself useful about the place. Then the quarry was closed because of the declining trade, and the machinery was sold, and the buildings started to fall down. But the two of them just stayed on. Caradoc Lloyd didn't mind. They weren't doing him any harm, and anyway Shechem had done odd jobs for him since he was a little boy. Protected them from the Council, he did. The Council! That was a business, seemingly. Persuaded the old lady to move into a council house. And she did – for about six weeks. Said she didn't like it. Felt shut in. So they just moved back, and I don't suppose the Council was that sorry since they never paid any rent. There was a social worker from Dolgellau wanted to move them after that. Said the cottage was insanitary. Sent them official letters. But Shechem never bothered to open them, not being able to read, so he says. And every time the poor man called the old lady just locked the door. Until, of course, he got tired of it, it being a long way from Dolgellau. So at last they sent the other man, some high-up official seemingly, and an Englishman as I told you. And he tried to throw his weight about, where the others had been gentle, see? – Said they'd have to go or he'd have them evicted. Big man, he was, and blond seemingly. Shechem nearly killed him – it was only Shechem's mother that saved the man. Of course there was an awful row, but it all died down in the end. Things have a way of doing that in the valleys, more's the pity. Anyway, Shechem hates foreigners that interfere – especially blond ones, and Englishmen.'

'I'm English, and blond – well more or less,' Septimus said.

'Aye. I'd noticed.' Dylan's grin was quite attractive, although Septimus did not entirely appreciate it.

'How do they live? Well, Shechem is marvellous with the sheep – he's good with all beasts, come to that. Seems to have an understanding with them. Perhaps he thinks like them.

The farmers say he's worth three sheep dogs, and they lose fewer sheep here than anywhere else on the mountains. If a ewe gets trapped, Shechem can tell by its crying; and when the ravens circle a sickly lamb, Shechem takes it up and rears it. So the farmers give him something. Then there's Caradoc Lloyd. And he fishes and poaches. I don't expect he does too badly, really. And at least he does not have to work in a factory, which would kill him for sure.' He fell silent and Septimus said, 'Well, you've told me all about Shechem. What about his mother?'

Dylan positively grinned at him. 'I don't know whether I will tell you anything about her, Mr Treloar.'

'Why?'

'Because you would only think I was a liar if I did.'

Septimus was wondering what to reply to this when he heard the clink and clatter of someone coming through the quarry.

'That will be Shechem now,' said Dylan, standing up. A moment, and then Septimus could hear a voice singing in Welsh. He recognized the tune. It was the hymn 'Loving Shepherd of Thy Sheep'. It seemed an appropriate signature tune for Sheep Shechem.

He came round the shoulder of the slate tip followed by a half-grown lamb. He stopped momentarily when he saw the two men, then came forward again, the lamb butting its head against his calf as if he was its mother. He was something of a surprise to Septimus. The man was a giant. No, not a giant. It was the breadth of shoulder that gave the illusion. He was not in fact quite as tall as Septimus, but he must be immensely strong. His face was deeply tanned, almost the colour of old oak, but it was quite unlined, a roundish face which had retained the innocent, unformed quality of the face of a very small child. Dark eyes gazed at Septimus with concentrated infantile curiosity. At the back of them, like glowing embers, there was a smouldering hostility. His hair was long and dark, and he was wearing a mudstained pair of corduroy trousers and a heavy black oilskin which had once belonged to the Merioneth County Council. The greeting between the two Welshmen was like the confluence of two mountain streams.

In the event, the interview was one of the least satisfactory he had ever conducted, only to be compared to one he had once had with an Indian Moslem who had been stabbed in a pub brawl. That had been conducted through an interpreter, and it had been some time before he discovered that the Indian thought he was being arrested for being in the public house and drinking alcohol, rather than being questioned as the victim of a stabbing which he seemed to think he richly deserved. There was the same lack of relation between Septimus's questions and Shechem's answers. It was as if they inhabited two different civilizations with totally different moral values and laws. Had Shechem ever been fishing from Hugh-ap-Lloyd's altar? The question and answer were duly translated by Dylan, who was obviously all set to enjoy the encounter between the two worlds.

'He says he never goes fishing because it is cruel to the fish, and anyway there are only eels in the Afon Maenen.'

Septimus produced the things he had found on the rock. 'Tell him I know he goes fishing, and that these belong to him, and that I found them on the altar rock.'

Once again the laborious translation and the flood of liquid Welsh in reply.

'He says that Caradoc Lloyd of the Plas allows him to fish, so you cannot lock him up for that.'

'Lord!' thought Septimus, 'this is going to take a week.'

In the event it took about forty minutes.

Shechem, after denying that he fished, denied that he fished in the Afon Maenen, that he had cut down the fir tree or crossed it. Then quite suddenly he admitted that he had seen the dead trout on the altar stone. No, he had not been there, he had just seen it.

He was more forthcoming about the gull. Yes, he had seen the fire. He had been coming back late from the mountain top where he had been looking for one of Pandy Harris's rams called Conqueror. No, he had not gone to investigate. He was afraid of the ghosts round the ruined chapel. Yes, there were ghosts. And in other magic places on the hills. He would not say where else he had seen ghosts, but after five minutes' evasion suddenly admitted that he had seen them on the pillar and by the cave.

At this point Dylan proffered some advice. 'Do not ask where the cave is, Mr Treloar. It is a secret which he will not divulge, and he will probably just go into the house and lock the door.' Septimus left the point, with a mental note to take it up later with Dylan.

Reluctantly Shechem admitted that at least one of the ghosts he had seen had been that of Hugh-ap-Lloyd. He had known him by his wizard's hat. Yes, there were a lot of lambs on the mountain. He had raised twelve himself. Owen Evans was very pleased and had given him a sack of potatoes, two blankets, a piece of bacon and some cigarettes. Yes, some of the lambs were black. Septimus could see them for himself in the enclosure. No, there was nothing special about black lambs.

At last Septimus sighed and climbed stiffly to his feet. He was tired with concentrating on what had been said and the nuances of what had not been said, and his behind appeared to have turned into a lump of slate. 'It was worth it,' he thought, 'even if I do get piles.'

'Will you thank him?' he said to Dylan. 'Tell him his information has been very helpful.' He produced a 50p piece and pressed it into Shechem's hand. They watched him walk towards the cottage. The window curtain twitched and the door opened, apparently by magic, since Shechem's mother was keeping out of sight. At the door Shechem turned, and called to them. The words had a rhythm which made them sound like a piece of verse. Then he went into the cottage, still followed by the lamb. The door closed softly and there was the sound of the bolts being thrust home. The curtain twitched again, and there was the white face peering out at them.

They slogged up the path in silence, Septimus leading. At the top of the incline he paused for breath, looking out over the panorama of lakes and mountains.

'What was that Shechem said at the door?' asked Septimus. 'It sounded like a rhyme.'

'It was a rhyme,' Dylan replied. 'Sort of. An old spell really.'

'A spell?'

'Yes. He knows all sorts of spells. Spells for curing warts and finding bees, charms for making your ewes have twins.'

'I see,' Septimus said. 'And does he use them?'

'He doesn't, but his mother does. She's what you would call a witch.' Septimus looked at him, noting the suppressed mirth, taking the information quite calmly. He was now beyond being surprised.

'So she's a witch. I suppose that was what you wouldn't tell me about her?'

'I didn't think you would believe it,' said Dylan. 'Do you?'

'I can be persuaded to believe anything,' Septimus replied.

'Not broomsticks and a black cat and a pointed hat,' said Dylan. 'A white witch. She can cure things. You would be surprised.'

Septimus noted that the young man was quite serious. He understood the sensitivity that made Dylan afraid of the derision of a much older man. He guessed that Dylan had probably had some personal experience of the woman's supposed powers, and he was wise and humble enough to recognize that there were skills and powers that a technological civilization could not explain. In his long career he had come across them, though trickery was the usual explanation.

'And what was this spell that he recited?' he asked.

A guarded look crossed Dylan's face. Was it the fear of being disbelieved again, or was it something more?

'It's too difficult to translate,' he said.

'You can always try.'

'It doesn't really mean anything.'

'Let's hear it.'

Dylan paused, selecting words, then answered flatly, 'It's a rhyme the children recite, a sort of nursery rhyme, like "Ring-a-roses".'

Septimus remembered that 'Ring-a-roses' was rather more than just a nursery rhyme, since it referred to the symptoms of the plague.

'I cannot give you the metre of course, but it runs something like this:

> *'A white bird and a silver fish,*
> *A black lamb and a white child,*
> *To help on Mother's washing day.'*

8

The Black Lamb

Septimus was sitting with his back against a rock looking down to Llyn Barlwyd. He could see the track up which he and Dylan had come after the interview with Shechem. He could see the chimney of Shechem's cottage, a trail of smoke coming from it. There was the Plas where Caradoc Lloyd lived – a modest house for all its grand name. The light was beginning to go, and the valley was beginning to fill with darkness like flowing ink.

It was a full hour since he had parted from Dylan, sending him on alone, saying he wished to stay on the mountainside and think. Dylan had been curiously unwilling to leave him, but Septimus had been insistent so the young man had gone on alone. He certainly needed to think. The investigation had quite suddenly taken a much more serious twist. Up to now he had viewed it as a rather macabre sort of joke which irritated his professional curiosity like a stone in a shoe. But now? A white bird and a silver fish, a black lamb . . . and a white child. Child sacrifice simply did not happen in the twentieth century. It belonged to the barbaric past! Grimly he reminded himself that it did happen in the twentieth century. Witchcraft and voodoo and sadism. Without difficulty he could call to mind half a dozen cases which had made screaming newspaper headlines over the last quarter of a century. Sitting there, watching the dusk shroud the Welsh countryside with the blanket of the dark he reminded himself that at that moment there were people in prison for the ritual murder of children. It did happen, and, for all the comic associations of the case, it could happen here. But what could he do? He had no evidence, not real evidence to convince an overworked police department. Wryly he acknowledged what his own reactions would have been had an elderly parson turned up with such a tale. He was on his own. Grimly, he set about marshalling his facts.

Clearly if someone was trying to work out the details of Hugh-ap-Lloyd's piece of magic in the Red Book, there were three things to be said about him (or her? He must get to see Shechem's mother). First, it was someone who felt passionately about the sanctity of the valley and who was prepared to go to any lengths to protect it. Second, it was someone who could really believe in the power of what, for the want of a better word, he would call witchcraft. The power of 'the old gods'. Third, it was someone who must be as mad as a hatter. Though madness was a relative term. 'There are more things, Septimus,' he muttered, 'than are dreamt of in a copper's philosophy.'

So he could rule out casual acts of vandalism. That left him with John Wesley Jones who certainly knew the legends

76

and who had spent at least one spell in a mental hospital. Then there was Dylan, who also knew the legends and was given to violence, but was much more likely to seek a political solution. He had known the rhyme which Shechem had quoted, and Septimus guessed that he had seen its relation to the Red Book and the sinister significance of the reference to the child. Did his father know the rhyme? Had he really been unable to translate those crucial sections of the Red Book or had he only been pretending? Then there was Sheep Shechem and his mother. They knew the rhyme, but did they know its possible connections? Did they know the Red Book? Could Shechem really read? It seemed unlikely. But then it was perfectly possible that the stories had been handed down in folklore, as bedtime stories for children. A white witch was the sort of person who would be likely to know such stories.

There was the unknown Caradoc Lloyd who owned the Red Book and knew more about it than anyone else and was supposedly descended from the wizard. Finally – Septimus faced reality – there were any number of other possible people whom he did not know about at all.

He stood up stiffly. It was nearly dark now. He had no idea how long he had been sitting. His watch had stopped and he realized that he was very hungry. It seemed a long time since lunch. He set off across the watershed between the two valleys, and as he started to descend the other side he remembered Hugh-ap-Lloyd's cave which Shechem had been so reluctant to talk about. Dylan had explained. 'Shechem thinks of it as a secret and magical place, and therefore a dangerous place, and to talk of it is to give it power over you.' Septimus remembered the Biblical fear of using the name of a god. 'Because he is the son of his mother, he will not speak of it,' Dylan had said. 'It is dangerous to meddle with wizards. Really of course it is just a cave.' He had shown Septimus the track leading to it along the base of the Craig-y-Moch crags, a clear line trampled by the feet of the climbers

77

who used it for shelter. 'They spend the night in it sometimes,' Dylan had said. 'But Shechem would not do that.'

Septimus stood on the western edge of the watershed looking down at the track. He wanted to have a look at the cave, and with his new sense of urgency he wanted to do it tonight. But there was no approaching it from this end for at one point the cliffs fell sheer into the water of the lake. It had to be approached from the Craig-y-Moch quarry. It was lighter on this side of the mountain because it faced west, and the path looked plain enough, and there was a clear track leading along the top of the cliffs which connected with the fisherman's path by the Afon Maenen. Late though it was, he decided to risk it. He had a feeling, which he certainly could not have explained, but which was born of all the years of experience, that the whole strange business was moving to a climax.

In fact it took him nearly two hours, the distances being deceptive and the going often rough. When he came out of the trees which clung to the Afon the moon had risen behind him. He could see the glimmer of it on the lake and the shape of the mountains opposite, but because it was behind him, all this side of the valley was dark with the shadow of the massive Moelwyns. The track led over a shoulder and through another grove of stunted trees before coming out on the naked scree. It was very dark beneath the trees and the foliage was stirring restlessly, as if it were whispering of a coming storm. There seemed a malevolence about the trees, as if they resented his presence, as if they were intent on tripping him with their twisted roots.

He came out of the grove and stood a moment on the scree path. It seemed much lighter after the blackness under the trees, and he could see the path reasonably well, a black line curving away, climbing up the charcoal grey of the scree face. He moved out across the scree, the loose surface clattering beneath his feet, a loud, almost musical noise in the silence of the night. The track led steadily upward and

78

climbed steeply into a sharp ravine to pass between a pinnacle of rock and the cliff face. It was very dark between the
two faces of rock and Septimus was tempted to use the pencil
torch which, from old habit, he always carried. He rejected
the idea, not wishing to destroy his night vision.

He was halfway up the ravine when a little puff of cold
wind carried the smell to him. He stopped and sniffed the
air. The wind was blowing directly in his face, funnelled
between the rocks of the ravine. It was wood smoke, and in
it was an acrid component like a burning blanket and the
foul oily smell of burning meat.

He stood poised, listening intently, one hand on the rock
beside him, his head cocked on one side. He stood so, utterly
still, for several minutes, motionless as the rock against which
he was leaning. But there was no sound, not the slightest
glow to indicate a fire over the top of the little pass. Cautiously he moved on and upward. In such a place it was impossible
to move really silently, and the occasional clatter of stones
would be the clearest warning to anyone who might be in the
darkness ahead. If there was anyone there they would anyway have heard his approach along the path and would
certainly be ready for him. Much more likely they would
have escaped along the path. He reached the top of the
ravine and peered over, allowing only the top half of his head
to appear above the skyline. There was the cave mouth
scarcely twenty feet away, a black oval against the darkness
of the cliffs, the path rising to it then falling away and disappearing into the night along the foot of the rock face.

Once again he listened. The smell was stronger now, and
he fancied he could see a curl of smoke rising from the mouth
of the cave. But there was no glow of fire. He stood for a long
time, waiting and watching. There was no sound, not the
smallest movement in the black cave mouth. He analysed
sounds. There was the muted roar of the Afon behind him,
the lapping of water on the lake shore a hundred feet below.
The wind made little whispering and moaning noises among

the rocks, and somewhere in the far distance a cow was bellowing its unhappiness to the unheeding moon. So he stood. There was a soft rustle of wings close over his head, and an owl hooted once, seeing his motionless figure, and swooped away, and was gone in the night.

At last he moved slowly, carefully along the path, his arms hanging loose, his muscles tense and ready. He reached the cave mouth. It was about shoulder high and he had to steel his nerve to stoop and enter. He moved swiftly now, keeping close to the edge of the cave mouth, sliding in, his back to the rock so that he should not be silhouetted against the night. He stood just inside, his back against the rock, his head and shoulders bowed by the roof of the cave. If an attack were to come, it would surely come now. There was no movement, no sound. Slowly he relaxed. He took his pencil torch from his inside pocket. Its tiny beam was blinding white in the blackness. He shone the circle of light round the cave. It threw a pale grey circle on the blackness of the rock, varying in size and shape as it flicked along the uneven surface like a distorting mirror in a fun fair. The cave sloped to the back and ended in what seemed to be a fall of rock. He was convinced now. He must be alone. The torch would surely have produced a reaction from anyone hiding in the cave. He brought the circle of light down to the floor in the cave mouth and saw what he expected to see: the charred remains of a fire, the horrible, half-burnt carcase of a lamb, a slate dagger sticking from its breastbone. A white bird and a silver fish . . . and a black lamb. Ignoring his revulsion for the messy task, he pulled out the dagger, slipped it into his pocket, and stood a moment wiping his hands on his jacket. He had put the torch away for a moment and the blackness in the cave was total.

Out of the blackness there came a sudden rattle of stone. He tensed, moving softly back until he could feel the rock against his back. There was someone there! Possible courses of action flashed through his mind. Investigate with the torch? Desperately dangerous. Get out of the cave and wait? The attack came swiftly, silently and with the utmost ferocity. He was flung half across the cave and powerful fingers were clutching at his throat, fingernails digging into his flesh.

In a curiously detached way some disengaged part of his mind registered the fact that he could hardly breathe and that he had been winded in the fall, and that they were rolling across the remains of the fire. They fetched up with a bump against the far wall of the cave. Septimus's attacker was closest to the wall, a chance fact which saved Septimus's life.

His hands were clawing at the other man's wrists, but he might as well have clawed at steel bars. The blood was thundering in his head and he knew that he would very soon be unconscious. With a despairing effort he grasped the wrists and pulled the assailant forward and then thrust back with all his failing strength. There was a satisfactory thump as the man's head hit the cave wall. Momentarily the fingers round Septimus's throat relaxed and he heaved the wrists apart and rolled desperately away into the darkness. For a moment he saw his assailant outlined against the entrance to the cave. He looked like some enormous black bat. Then he was gone and Septimus was alone in the cave and the sound of jingling stone on the path faded into the distance. Septimus crawled to the cave mouth and peered out, but there was nothing to see, and he was too spent for pursuit, and anyway he had twisted his knee badly in the brief fight. He crawled into the open and sat on the path while he recovered. He was in considerable pain, but despite the pain he forced himself to think. He could put no description to his opponent except the silly phrase 'like a black bat', and that was not much use. There was the strength of the man. That ruled out Dylan. Wesley Jones and Shechem could certainly have done it, but he must be honest. It was impossible to gauge the real strength of an assailant who attacked with such sudden ferocity and such advantage of surprise. It was the ferocity that was so startling.

Was there anything else? His mind was clearer now. Yes, there was! His assailant had turned left at the cave mouth, not right, which was the direction from which Septimus had approached. Now when he had looked at the path with Dylan he had seen that it did not really lead anywhere. It was simply the path which the climbers used to reach the bottom of their routes up the cliff face. It came to an end where the rock face fell sheer into the lake. But there was a way down from the path to a tiny beach on the lake shore. Therefore it was very probable that his attacker had come by boat. He sat a moment longer considering routes and distances. It was at least two miles along the scree path, two difficult and dangerous miles in the darkness. The little beach was far down the lake from Hafod Maenen. There was the twisting path down to it to negotiate and then the long row back to the village. Normally it would be far quicker to walk the other way, down through the quarry and along the road at the head of the lake. He could have done it easily – but for his twisted knee. Well at least he could try. He heaved himself to his feet and set off at the best speed he could manage.

It was not an enjoyable journey. The twisted knee made him clumsy, and twice he fell. Each time he dragged himself grimly to his feet and pressed on. Along the scree path, down through the quarry, then limping swiftly along the road. He had hoped that he might see a boat on the lake, but the moon had gone behind the heavy clouds which were gathering over the mountains and it was too dark.

At last, dirty and battered, his clothes torn and his knee burning like fire, he came to Hafod Maenen. Beside the public phone box outside the Royal Stores stood the one street lamp that the village possessed. Septimus sat himself in a dark corner outside the Maenofferen Arms where the dim light from the lamp illuminated the road and the end of the path at the bottom of the Mill garden. The shop windows

82

opposite were dark, but there were lights in the upstairs rooms. A hum of conversation came from the bar of the Maenofferen Arms.

Septimus waited. His breathing came back to normal, leaving him only desperately weary.

A courting couple came out of the bar and turned right, moving away from Septimus towards the head of the lake. Their arms were round one another, their heads close together as they murmured softly in Welsh and disappeared into the darkness without a glance toward the bulky shadow in the corner. A man came out, followed by a dog. It was Sandy. He limped along the road in front of Septimus. He was humming a tune. He did not turn his head, and fortunately the wind was such that Pandy did not scent Septimus and come to investigate. Sandy disappeared, and a moment later there was a glow of light across the road from the kitchen window of the Mill.

Someone started to play the piano in the Maenofferen Arms, and the first scuds of rain swept across the road. Septimus began to wonder if his mad rush had been for nothing when he heard the sound of footsteps coming up from the lake. A figure emerged from the alley, plodding slowly, its back towards him; a man in waders with a fishing bag across his shoulders and cased rods in his hand. It was John Wesley Jones. Septimus got up and moved into the lamplight.

'Evening, John,' he said.

The other man turned, startled. He looked for a long moment and then said, 'Oh! It's Mr Treloar. Couldn't see for a minute. I was dazzled by the light. Evening to you.' He came a couple of paces towards Septimus and added, 'Goodness me! You been falling in more brambles then?' Septimus realized that he must look something of a mess. But then so did John Wesley Jones. His fishing coat was torn, his face scratched and muddy.

'Yes,' said Septimus evenly, 'I went for a walk and tripped in the dark. Getting clumsy in my old age. Suppose I should have taken a torch. You look as if you've had a fall yourself, John.'

The other man laughed. It was a selfconscious laugh with no mirth in it.

'Man!' he said. 'I've a real fisherman's tale about the one that got away. I was casting for a trout that was feeding under the trees on the far side of the llyn. I'd landed because the casting was easier – on account of the wind. You'll not believe it, but I hooked a salmon. Big one, I should think. Daren't put any weight on the trout tackle, so I followed him down the bank. Hundreds of yards – least it seemed like hundreds of yards. Then I fell over a rock. Broke my tackle. Didn't catch anything else either.'

'You'd better give up fishing and take up golf,' Septimus said.

Again the artificial laugh. 'Think I'll do that. Well, I'd better go and get cleaned up. So had you, Mr Treloar. Goodnight.'

Septimus bade him goodnight and watched him cross the road and go into the lane leading to his cottage.

Much later, after a bath and a supper by the fire, Septimus told Sandy the events of the day. The old soldier listened in silence, his hand on Pandy's head.

He grunted when Septimus had finished. 'Hmmm. Salmon rising in the lake? At night? In April?'

'Is it impossible?' Septimus asked.

'In fishing nothing's impossible, but at least I've never heard of it. Salmon do come through the lake, but not many and not often. The outfall's too shallow. But then John Wesley Jones could have thought up a more convincing story than that if he was lying.'

'Which makes the tall tale more believable,' said Septimus.

They fell silent a moment, listening to the rain scudding across the window.

'So you've got your black lamb,' said Sandy at length.

Septimus was listening to the storm. 'And as near as dammit got murdered for my pains,' he said. 'Hark to that, Sandy – the wind shouting in his strength and the lake rising like the sea.'

9

The White Witch

Septimus slipped out the clutch and jammed on the brakes of the Land-Rover. 'Oh, God!' he said, 'that's all I need.' It was the following morning, the storm had blown itself out, and Septimus was on his way round the lake to visit Hugh-ap-Lloyd's cave by daylight.

Dylan Wesley Jones was emerging from the lane leading to his home. His arm was in a sling and there was a swelling purple bruise on the side of his face.

'Morning!' Septimus shouted. 'And what happened to you?'

Dylan grinned lopsidedly. 'Been fighting, haven't I?' he said.

'And who have you been fighting this time?' Septimus was like an angry schoolmaster enthroned in the Land-Rover.

'Well, after I left you yesterday I met that surveyor. We finished our argument and he belted me with his theodolite.'

'Serve you damn well right,' said Septimus grimly and drove off. So now he had two injured suspects, and among all the things that had to be done with considerable urgency he must find the surveyor and check on Dylan's story.

Despite stiffness, sundry bruises and a knee that would hardly work, Septimus had risen at seven and achieved much before leaving the Mill. Swearing sporadically at the knee, he had shaved and made tea for Sandy and himself. Then he had rung his old friend and police colleague Sam Burroughs.

Sam had still been in bed, and from the weary usage of many years had only been a little grumpy at being phoned at such an ungodly hour. He had even managed to sound pleased when he realized that the caller was Septimus. Septimus had not attempted to tell him the whole story – it was too weird to explain over the phone – but Sam had suddenly sounded wide awake when he realized that Septimus had been fighting with a possible homicidal maniac. 'Septimus,' he had said, his voice full of genuine concern, 'you're too old for that sort of barney. Leave it to the locals.' Septimus smiled to himself. It was pleasant to remember Sam's concern. Actually he had replied abruptly, 'Too old yourself, you old fool.' Then Sam had agreed to get Harvey Shortcross, the tame police surgeon, to ring Septimus at the Mill. And that, since Septimus had long and bitter experience of trying to contact Harvey Shortcross, was a very great deal achieved. 'Take care of yourself, Septimus old son,' Sam had said, and so had rung off.

Then May Parry and Gwyn had arrived, and the little boy had come to him and sat on his knee, watching entranced while Septimus had made a whole range of animals by knotting the washing-up cloth. It was a skill he had deliberately learned when he was a constable. It had been a sure-fire success with lost and frightened children. Now he used it with a certain guilty guile, keeping May Parry's mind off the significance of all the questions he was asking about John Wesley Jones. By the time breakfast was ready he had extracted all the information he could for his forthcoming conversation with the fiery Harvey Shortcross who abominated inaccuracy. Finally over bacon and egg he had impressed on Sandy the urgent necessity of an early meeting with Caradoc Lloyd, and Sandy had agreed to ring and fix something up.

He parked the Land-Rover by the Maenofferen Chapel

86

and went up through the quarry and along the path. It all seemed very steep and his knee pained him a good deal.

'Some fools are old fools,' he said to a startled sheep.

'Baaa!' said the sheep.

'I quite agree,' said Septimus. 'I ought to have broken my neck.'

He came to the cave, and so far as he could judge, nothing had been touched since the fight. It took him some moments to find sufficient unburnt wool to be sure that the revolting remains had once been a black lamb. He moved carefully round the cave, inspecting all the nooks and crannies with the aid of the big torch from the Land-Rover. There were signs of occupation by rock-climbers. In one corner he unearthed a cache of old tins, and he spent some time deciphering the graffiti scratched on the walls. 'Jock loves Fifi.' 'Adolf was Here.' And the mysterious inscription, 'Haggis climbed the Spider.' 'Curious baptismal name,' murmured Septimus as he continued his inspection.

He found nothing of note, except the nook in which his assailant had crouched. As he had noted by the light of his pencil torch, the cave sloped to the back, grew lower and ended in a pile of broken rock. He could not tell whether it was a natural fall or whether at some time the cave had been blocked off for reasons of safety. He went back to the entrance, stepping carefully over the pathetic and disgusting remains of the lamb. He looked back at it. It seemed even more revolting than the fish or the bird – probably because it was a mammal and bigger. He went outside, found a stout piece of slate, scraped a shallow grave and buried the remains of the animal.

When he had finished he turned left along the scree path and followed it below the cliffs until he scrambled down to the little beach. There were signs of boats having landed there, but when, there was no means of telling. It was as he came back up that he noticed the hole in the mountainside. It was at the point where the scree path ended. It was not large and it was half hidden by a big rock. He scrambled up to it. The bottom half of the hole was blocked with a breast-work of broken stone, neatly made as if the hole had been deliberately blocked and then at some later stage partially re-opened. He leaned over the breastwork. It was black inside and echoed to his shout, his voice going away and away reverberating into the heart of the mountain. Presumably it was a ventilation shaft, or some other sort of boring to do with the slate workings that riddled the mountain. Certainly it did not look inviting, and he shuddered at the thought of going into it. But this was the direction in which his assailant had come. So which way had he gone at this point? Down to the lake, or into the hole? Certainly he could have gone nowhere else – unless he had ropes and a com-panion and had climbed the cliff, and that was unthinkable in the dark.

When he got back to the Mill there was a note from Sandy on the kitchen table.

'I need various supplies, so as you will want the Land-Rover I have gone into Portmadoc with the Parrys on their trip to the wholesaler. Regular family party.

'Sam Burroughs rang. Your sawbones friend is sawing bones all day, so you are to ring him tonight – 01/594/63852 – at 8.0 p.m. You'll have to do it from the Plas because you are dining with Caradoc Lloyd at 7.0 p.m. Lunch in the fridge. Sandy.'

Septimus found himself a pie and an apple and a bottle of beer and went and sat on the parapet of the water-wheel looking out over the lake. The previous night's storm had blown itself out, but once again the weather was threatening, the clouds low over the mountains. Wise in the ways of weather, Septimus guessed it was a characteristic pattern. A series of depressions coming one after another from the empty spaces of the Atlantic. The storm would rise and fall and go on doing so until the overall weather pattern changed. It would rain and blow hard again before nightfall.

There was someone fishing on the far side of the lake under the shadow of Craig-y-Moch. The distance was too great to be sure who it was, so Septimus went into the Mill and found Sandy's binoculars. It was John Wesley Jones and he had little Gwyn Parry in the boat with him. Septimus frowned, the binoculars resting on his knee. He wished Sandy's 'family party' to the wholesaler in Portmadoc had included Gwyn — at least until he had talked to Harvey Shortcross. Then the very banality of the situation took hold of him. A little boy in a boat with a fisherman, his 'uncle'. It was so difficult to believe that there was any danger in it. Fishing was such an innocent occupation. He stood up, and the twinge of pain in his knee reminded him that the fight in the cave had been real enough, dangerous enough. Still, there was nothing he could do until he had talked to Harvey. He made up his mind and went back into the Mill. It was a decision he was later to regret.

He got out of the Land-Rover and drove down to the bottom of the lake. There was no one in sight, but the hut door was open. He knocked and stuck his head round the door. The Welsh surveyor with the Midlands accent was sitting reading a paper, his feet on a rough deal table.

'Hullo!' he said, surprised, sounding a little guilty. He removed his feet. 'Just having my dinner,' he said. He did not look as if he had been in a fight.

Septimus was at his most friendly, like a blue-eyed and sleepy bear on a hot afternoon.

'Just thought I'd drop in to apologize for my friend yesterday. I really was most ashamed of the way he behaved.'

'That's all right,' said the surveyor. 'You get used to it in this sort of job. They all want electricity, but when it comes to producing it, they don't want to know. Sit down, Mister.'

Septimus upended a box and took out his pipe. 'Smoke?' he said, proffering his pouch, having noted the surveyor's pipe on the table. The offer was accepted and the two men talked. Septimus discovered that the surveyor came from the

Rhondda. 'My father died in a pit accident. Oh, not the sort that gets reported on the telly. A lump of coal fell on his head, only it was too big a lump. There were four of us and no work, except in the pits. "You'll not work in the mine," my mam said. So when I grew up I went to Wolverhampton and ended up as a surveyor for the Electricity Board. I can understand how your friend feels. But what's the use, I say.' Septimus discovered that he had indeed met Dylan again on the previous afternoon. According to the surveyor they had not fought, just continued their argument.

'Well, he did try to go for me, but I just stepped back and he tripped over a rock. So I got in my car and drove back to my digs. He looked all right to me. Could have blacked his eye and hurt his arm, I suppose. But I never hit him with the theodolite whatever he may have told you.'

Septimus tapped out his pipe and took his leave. He was a good deal wiser about the problems of Welsh employment, but whether the surveyor was telling the truth about his meeting with Dylan or just covering himself against possible legal action Septimus could not say. So he was no further on in eliminating Dylan as a suspect.

He drove on, down the steep road out of the valley, around a series of precipitous hairpin bends and so came to the flat, fertile pasture of the estuary. He dropped a thousand feet in perhaps eight miles and found that spring had advanced a month, the lambs in the river meadows larger than their mountain kindred, the rhododendrons and azaleas already in bud and bursting into flower.

He drove along the main road, curving along beside the river, a road blessedly empty of holiday-makers. So he came to the lane leading up into Cwm Barlwyd, a narrow, twisting lane, climbing steeply between dry-stone walls wide enough for only one vehicle and with few passing places. And as the Land-Rover climbed, thundering in low gear, so the wind sharpened and the spring went back three weeks. He passed through the shallow ford where the lake drained out of the valley and on to the level rutted track that ran along the lake shore. At the far end he could see the Plas and beyond it the grey-blue jumble of the quarry with a smudge of white smoke from Shechem's cottage. He drove slowly now, for the track was unsurfaced and deeply pot-holed, no maintenance having been done on it for years. He parked the Land-Rover where the track started to climb sharply into the quarry, driving it tidily into a man-made cutting as if it might constitute a traffic hazard if he left it on the road. The engine died under his hand and he relished the silence – the crying of the sheep, the wind hissing in the reeds at the end of the lake, the distant crying of two ravens circling high over the mountainside.

He sat for a while in the driving seat considering exactly what he was going to do. He took out his pocket book, wrote a short note in block capitals, criticized it, and tore it up. Sheep Shechem's mother might well be baffled by the word 'professional'. He made several attempts before he was satisfied, rejecting 'ligament', 'consult' and 'accident'. His final version read, 'John Wesley Jones sent me. He says you can cure my twisted knee.' He limped up the track into the quarry. There might be some doubt about the truth of his message, there was certainly none about his damaged knee. The cottage and its surrounds were as they had been – the muddy donkey, the sow and piglets, the lambs, the ducks dabbling in the mud. Queen Victoria's bicycle stood beneath the window in the cluttered yard; Septimus noted that it was propped the other way round. He knocked at the cottage door and stepped back, looking at the window. As he expected, the curtains twitched and momentarily he saw the white face of the old lady. The door did not open.

He went back to the door. There was no letter box. 'Mother,' he called, 'I have a message for you.' Carefully he pushed his note under the door and then went and propped himself on the saddle of the vintage motor-cycle, taking his pipe from his pocket, watching the slip of white on the slate threshold. The piece of paper vanished. Septimus waited, puffing his pipe. With a clash of bolts the door opened and a woman's voice said, 'Come in, Mr Treloar.' It was a deep, well-modulated voice, not what Septimus had been expecting. He was a little surprised that the old lady even knew his name. Presumably she must have got that from Shechem. He knocked out his pipe and went into the cottage.

It was so dark, and the old lady was standing so deep in the shadows, that at first he could get no idea of what she was like. The window was so heavily curtained that most of the light came from the fire glowing in the hearth. She closed the door behind him and waited, saying nothing. Slowly his eyes adjusted to the gloom. The floor was slate, without any covering, the walls were unplastered blocks of slate. Open tread steps without handrail led to the floor above. Against one wall was a massive dresser full from floor to ceiling with boxes and jars. Herbs hung from the low rafters, bunches of leaves and berries and roots which he could not begin to name.

The old woman was tiny – so tiny that it was difficult to realize that she was the mother of the massive Shechem. She was dressed in voluminous clothes of black, a shawl over her head so that it was difficult to see anything of her face. Incongruously she made Septimus think of Queen Victoria. At least the image suited the elderly bicycle outside the window.

'John Wesley Jones did not send you,' she said. 'He would send no one to me. He is a preacher. He once called me the Witch of Endor in Bethesda Chapel. Why have you come, and why did you lie?'

'I lied,' said Septimus, 'because I wanted to see you. John Wesley Jones did tell me that you are skilled in healing.'

'You are the Englishman who was asking questions of Shechem.'

'Yes.'

'Why were you asking questions?'

Septimus found it a little unnerving to be questioned thus

abruptly when he had been intending to do the questioning himself. But it seemed best to give straightforward answers.

'Because there have been strange happenings on the mountains at night. I wondered if Shechem had seen anything.'

'Sit down,' she said. 'Let us look at this knee of yours.'

Obediently Septimus sat on an upright chair and rolled up his trouser leg. She knelt before him on the slate floor and explored the swollen knee. She seemed to need no more light than the glow of the fire. Her fingers were strong and competent, like the fingers of a surgeon.

'Ouch!' he said loudly and earnestly as the unerring fingers went to the most sensitive spot.

'You have strained the ligament,' she said. She sounded like a family doctor, and Septimus recalled the trouble he had taken over the note and mentally apologized for being so arrogant.

'Can you heal it?' he asked.

'I can ease the pain. But why should I?'

That was a good question, Septimus thought – since he had come, not for healing, but for information. Why indeed should she?

'Because you are a healer,' he said.

She went to the dresser and came back with an ointment which she smeared on the knee. It had a pungent smell which filled the room and tingled on the flesh like an after-shave lotion. She started to massage the knee with long, even strokes, her powerful fingers following the complicated contours of the bones under the puffy flesh. It was extremely painful, but Septimus did his best to ignore the pain, trying to keep his mind on the things he wished to find out. Where was Shechem? Had he been fighting? Why had he quoted the rhyme? As he thought of the rhyme the old woman spoke in Welsh. Septimus recognized the words and for a moment was so startled that he really forgot the pain in his knee. As he had been thinking of the rhyme about the fish and the bird, the lamb and the white child, so she had quoted it. It

93

was an eerie, an unnerving experience – as if there was an unsuspected window in his mind and this old woman with the white face and the powerful fingers was able to peer through it. He gathered his wits, saying nothing for a moment, and then he asked, as casually as he could, 'What is that?'

'Why do you lie?' she asked, but without emotion. 'You know what it is. It was not in this room before you came. It came to my mind from your mind.'

'I am sorry,' he said, 'I should not have lied. Yes, I do know it. Your son quoted it to me yesterday.'

'Then you know the Welsh?' She paused in her massaging and looked up at him, black eyes in a white face like the holes in a skull. She was surprised. It was the first emotion she had shown.

'No,' he replied, 'Dylan translated it for me.'

'Then why are you afraid because of a nursery rhyme?'

'How do you know I am afraid?'

'Even a dog knows when a man is afraid. But it is not for yourself you fear. What is it you fear?'

Septimus put the question aside. 'Let me ask you something first. Has the rhyme any meaning?'

'Meaning?' she said. 'It has as much meaning as any child's rhyme. It is a skipping game the girls play.'

Septimus had been able to detect no hesitation in her reply, but even so he could not tell whether she was speaking the truth.

'And what is it you fear?' she asked again.

He paused before replying, choosing the words carefully. 'That someone will do a great evil, believing that good will come of it.'

'A great evil,' she said. 'You fear that there will be death.'

'How do you know that?'

'If the bullock being led to the slaughter fears the death of which it has no knowledge, should I not know?'

'I fought a man for my life last night.'

'That I also know. And you were burnt in a fire.'

94

'How do you know that?'

She looked up at him again, and he could see even in that dim light that she was smiling. 'There is the smell of fire on your clothes, and your trousers are singed.'

'Where is Shechem?' he asked.

'You think it is Shechem whom you fought?'

'I do not think. I wish to find out. Where is Shechem?'

She stood up. 'There,' she said. 'Your knee will heal now, and quickly.'

'Thank you, mother. Where is Shechem?'

'Somewhere on the mountain. He did not come home last night. He often does not come home for days at a time.' It was oddly difficult to believe that she was lying.

'Do you not worry?' he asked.

'Worry? Why should I worry? Shechem is a child of the mountains. He is where he would be with the sheep and the ravens. If he has been fighting I shall know when he comes home.'

'If he has been fighting,' said Septimus, 'will you tell me?'

'It is foolish,' she said, 'to say I will do this or that. The future is what shall be. How do I know what I will do? Not even the very wise can see all the future. But if it seems good that you should know, when the time comes I will tell Caradoc Lloyd at the Plas and he will tell you on the telephone.'

Septimus thought for a moment, and then, 'Mother,' he said, 'I told you I am afraid of a great evil, though I do not clearly know what it is I fear. You know things. Do you know what it is I am afraid of?' She turned away from him and gazed into the fire.

'You are afraid that Shechem is trying to fulfil the old promises, and that the promises do not end with fish and birds and lambs.'

'Yes. I am afraid of that,' he said. 'What of you?'

'I do not know. But—yes. The fear has come to me.'

'Then why do you not act?'

She looked up at him and smiled. 'What would you have

95

me do? Lock him in his bedroom as if he was a little child?'

'You could always go to the police,' he suggested, desperately.

'Police!' She repeated the word, and in that strange atmosphere it was like an alien visitor from another planet. 'And what should I tell the police? That my son believes in the old gods? That he hates all who would change the valleys as I hate them myself? That he does not think as they think? That there are legends and tales? And all they could do would be to lock him up, and that would be death for him, a death such as I would not give to the very mountain fox that raids my hens. But I will do as I said. I will tell Caradoc Lloyd if there is anything to tell, and he will tell you. Now you will leave me, for there is nothing more to say.'

And with that, Septimus had, perforce, to be content.

'Thank you,' he said. 'And thank you for attending to my knee. I must pay you for that.' He reached for his wallet, but she forestalled him, her hand held up, palm foremost, as if she were giving a blessing.

'No. I will accept no payment for treating you. You are a good man, and it is good that you try to do.'

'Thank you, mother. That is kind. But I am not a good man. I have lived among evil all my life.'

'That is why you are good,' she said, 'for the evil has not touched you. But – for payment – be gentle with my Shechem if he has strayed from the paths of wisdom. And go in peace.'

To this Septimus could find no reply. He bowed his head and walked from the cottage, puzzled and humbled. In all his wide experience he had never met anyone more extraordinary than the old woman. He heard the door shut and the bolts pushed home, but he did not look back. He had rarely disliked himself so much.

10

Dinner at the Plas

It was a full hour before he was due at the Plas, so he climbed slowly up through the quarry, noting without surprise that his knee was already a great deal easier. He sat, looking down into the valley, and tried to make sense of his extraordinary interview with Shechem's mother.

That she was telling the truth as she understood it, he was morally certain. He dimly understood that her ways of looking at things, her ideas of good and evil, of truth and falsehood, were far different from the modes of perception of a technological world. Both a machine and a torrent could cut a ravine in a mountain. But the machine imposed its will by an alien geometry of power and steel, whereas the way of the torrent was the slow way of co-operation. Morality, he saw, could be the same – systems imposed from outside, a rigid scale to which nature must be made to conform. But if you did not conform, if like the sapling you bent with the wind? Nature, he reminded himself grimly, was not all mountain streams and roses, it was – as the old platitude truly said – 'red in tooth and claw'. One could look at nature and accept the doctrine 'what will be – will be'. One could accept it sometimes. Now, for instance. Sitting here looking down at a placid lake with the cry of the sheep on the lonely mountain. But what about when the cat was tormenting a bird it had caught, or a raven attacking a lamb? He thought of the food chain of the predators, of life preying on life, and for a

97

moment it seemed that there could be no God, or only a mindless evil organizing creation to produce the maximum of blood and fear and suffering. He deliberately turned his mind from the philosophical speculation. Certainly Shechem's mother belonged to an older, perhaps wiser, certainly more intuitive world, but did she know the sinister interpretation of the rhyme? Did she suspect her son? He smiled wryly. 'Suspect' was a policeman's word, smacking of clues and interrogations and identity parades. It would not come into her world view. 'Does the turkey suspect the farmer's wife in the days before Christmas?' he said softly and sarcastically. Then his practical policeman's instincts forced him to recognize that the whole episode could have been a gigantic con, with Shechem upstairs, recovering from the fight, and listening to every word of the conversation. It could be. Only he did not think it was.

As he cogitated he was looking down at the little cottage. It looked agreeably snug with its smoking chimney and attendant livestock in that place of great loneliness. The door of the cottage opened and Shechem's mother came out. She was wearing what appeared to be a red mackintosh over her voluminous garments and she was carrying a shopping basket. She put the basket into its companion on the front of Queen Victoria's bicycle and rode down the track by the lake, wobbling from side to side as she went. Septimus smiled, thinking of Queen Victoria, and recognizing in himself a queer affection for the strange old woman. He was mildly curious to know where she was going since it was far too late for a shopping trip. He watched her until she was a tiny figure at the far end of the lake, an insect among the grandeur of the hills. She got off her bicycle and laid it in the bracken. Then she stooped, doing something around her legs. It was too far to see, but he guessed and laughed aloud as she crossed the path and waded into the reedy shallows. She had taken off her boots and tucked up her skirts. She moved slowly out, shopping basket in hand. Presumably she was gathering herbs for her healing craft. He stood up and started to walk back down the track, wondering as he did so whether she was renewing her stock of whatever it was she had used on his knee.

He was not proud of what he proposed to do. 'The evil has not touched you.' He quoted the old woman's words a little bitterly to himself. Then, remembering the steely fingers that had clutched at his throat, he put the paralysing cynicism aside. A black lamb could be followed by a white child.

He took the key from under the stone by the dovecote, unlocked the door and went into the cottage.

He might as well not have troubled his conscience, for he learnt little from the cottage. The fire had been banked down, and he left the door open to improve the light. The room was as it had been: table, chairs, dresser, drying herbs hanging from the rafters. He went to the dresser and looked uncomprehendingly at the pots and jars, the unrecognizable seeds and leaves. On the dresser-top was a row of books, a massive, calf-bound folio doing duty as a bookend. It was a Welsh Bible, dated 1820, the end-papers filled with a record of births and deaths. Jones's and Lloyds and Evans's, with the Christian name Shechem appearing like a minor theme in a symphony. The rest of the books was a fascinating collection, and Septimus guessed that, had they been auctioned at Sothebys, they would have made Shechem and his mother rich for life. They were all in Welsh and mostly in manuscript. The earliest date that Septimus could find was 1620, but some of the books looked older than that. The most recent was in manuscript and had been started in 1923. Each entry was dated, and the hand was the same, becoming smaller and more crabbed as the years lengthened. The most recent entry was dated three months previously. The entries looked like recipes, and Septimus guessed that it was the old woman's personal herbal. He left the books and went softly up the loft ladder to the bedroom.

Here there was practically nothing. Two beds with coarse

blankets and sheepskins but no sheets, by each bed an apple box, a tin candlestick and a match box on the top, a few clothes hanging on nails driven into the raw slate wall – there was nothing else but a picture. It was a very old photograph of a group of bearded quarrymen standing selfconsciously by an enormous lump of slate. The frame was coming apart and the glass was cracked.

Septimus went softly down the stairs, locked the cottage door and put the key back under the stone. He noticed that the second cottage in the row, though derelict, still had part of its roof and a rudimentary door of salvaged planking. He pushed the door open and went in. The room had been fitted out as a very rough workshop. There was a primitive bench beneath the hole where there had once been a window on the back wall. It was littered with files and saws, and everything was covered with a fine powdering of slate dust. On a shelf beside the bench was a number of slate ornaments – ash trays, rough bases for table lamps, slate fans and paper knives. So Sheep Shechem also made things for the tourist trade. No one had told him about that. But then, for men who had grown up with slate it would seem so ordinary as not to be worth mentioning, and the paper knives were flimsy things, not in the least like the wicked and purposeful daggers he had in his possession. Certainly, Shechem was capable of making the weapons, but he would hardly leave them among his tourist stock. Septimus was wandering around the workshop looking for possible places of concealment when he heard the distant clink of slate. Someone was coming down through the quarry. He went swiftly to the door and peeped through one of the gaps between the ill-fitting planks. Although the light was beginning to go it was easy to identify Shechem's bulky outline and his swift, free-ranging stride.

Septimus considered a moment, tense, poised for action. The workshop was in full view from the track, so there was no going through the door. Hastily he turned back into the room, clambered on to the bench and out through the hole where the window had been. Behind the row of cottages the land fell steeply to the stream, so he had to drop about six feet, landing clumsily in a bed of nettles, suppressing curses as the nettles reacted to his presence. He wriggled close to the cottage wall and lay still. He remembered that the Romans were supposed to have introduced the nettle to Britain for medicinal purposes. He would have things to say to Julius Caesar if they ever met hereafter.

He heard the sound of boots in the yard, then the workshop door opened, and he could hear Shechem moving about above him. He was talking to himself and humming snatches of a song. Septimus knew himself to be safe enough, unless Shechem suspected his presence and leaned right out of the hole above the bench. He heard the workshop door close, and a moment later Shechem went into the cottage. He waited for a moment or two, then crept cautiously down the ravine, between the bed of nettles and the cottage wall. It was difficult going, not only because of the nettles, but because of the rubbish which, over the years, had been thrown into the ravine. Once he sent a rusting tin clattering and rattling into the stream, and he lay still wondering what he would do if Shechem heard and came to investigate. But nothing happened, so he moved on and so came out below the cottages and over the bank to where he had parked the Land-Rover.

He climbed into the vehicle and with handkerchief and car duster did what he could to clean his person and his clothes. On this particular job he seemed to spend his time falling into things. He was nearly due at the Plas, but he would dearly love to get a look at Shechem to see if he showed any signs of the fight. He debated possibilities. He could go and knock at the cottage door, but Shechem would almost certainly refuse to open it, and anyway he was unwilling to disclose his presence in the valley. He was still arguing the question with himself when once again he heard the sound of someone on the slate track. He went and stood in the middle of the lane. It was Shechem. He was setting off into the hills again. Septimus was perturbed, although he could not give real substance to his fears. Anyway, there was nothing he could do. He returned to the Land-Rover and drove round to the Plas.

Caradoc Lloyd met him at the door, a big man, taller than Septimus but with a stoop. The flesh was stretched taut over his frame, and he had a big nose and receding hair so that he looked like an elderly eagle. 'I saw you coming round the end of the llyn,' he said, and led the way into the house.

They drank sherry in a small study looking out across the dark lake to the last angry glow of the sun setting behind the clouds over the Irish Sea. A woman came in carrying an oil lamp and the room was flooded with a soft golden light. With easy courtesy Caradoc Lloyd performed introductions.

'The Reverend Septimus Treloar. This is Mrs Harris who keeps house for me.'

Mrs Harris closed the door softly behind her and Septimus looked round the room in the lamp glow. It was lined from floor to ceiling with books, and the fireplace was a delicately carved affair of blue slate.

'And now, Mr Treloar, before we dine, what can I do for you? Colonel Sanderson would not go into details, but I gathered that it is a matter which might be of some importance.'

'It is very difficult to explain,' said Septimus, 'and I don't want to go into more details than I've got to, because it's mostly supposition, but I gather from Sandy that you are the authority on the Red Book.'

'Yes,' said the other man, 'I suppose I am. It is the family's greatest treasure, and I have devoted a somewhat idle life to the study of early Welsh history. Such knowledge as I have is at your service.'

Septimus told him briefly and as unemotionally as possible of the fish, the bird and the lamb.

'I see,' said Caradoc Lloyd gravely, when he had finished.

'So you think someone is re-enacting that particular story from the Red Book?'

'It seems likely,' said Septimus.

'If that is true, then you do well to take it with the utmost seriousness. You Englishmen — forgive me for the impertinence, Mr Treloar — but you English have never understood the Welsh. Perhaps you have never tried because you think of us as Englishmen with a different accent. But we are not. We are Celts. We have more in common with Brittany and the Western Isles and Ireland than we have with Herefordshire.'

'And Cornwall,' Septimus murmured.

'Quite so. By your name I guessed you were Cornish, so perhaps you can appreciate the difference.'

'I'm better at it than I was a week ago,' Septimus answered.

'The Celts are the myth-makers. Arthur and Gawain, Merlin and Morgan-le-Fay, and a great many more besides.'

'But they are myths,' said Septimus. 'Merlin is supposed to be asleep somewhere in a cave, but who goes looking for him in the twentieth century?'

'But Mr Treloar, the power of the myth lies not in the truth of the original fact. It lies in the belief of those who listen to the myth. It is like the witch-doctors of primitive tribes. Do you die because of the spell he casts, or the poison he administers, or because you believe you will die? You die all the same. The old tales are part of the Celtic blood, and if someone is indeed trying to make that particular story come true I would view the matter with the utmost gravity . . . the utmost gravity.'

A gong sounded in the hall and Caradoc Lloyd got to his feet. 'Come, Mr Treloar, let us dine.' He collected a leatherbound quarto volume from one of the bookcases as they went to the door.

He put the book down on the oval dining table. 'This is my typescript translation of the Red Book,' he said, 'the single

fruit of a misspent life. I do not say it is absolutely correct –
John Wesley Jones was quite right about the obscurity of the
language – but it is accurate enough for your purposes.' He
spooned up soup with one hand, turning the pages of the
book with the other. 'Ah! Here we are.' He put his spoon down.

'Here is the bit that Wesley Jones could not translate. You
get the business about the bird and the fish, and then this –
"Hugh-ap-Lloyd took the black lamb of the white ewe and
offered it with the sword of the new faith on the very threshold of the last citadel. And the wind shouted in his strength,
and the torrent tumbled the rock, and the lake rose like the
sea, and the invader was greatly afraid that the gods would
wake. Then Ifan Ddu laughed. 'The old gods sleep too
deep for your awakening,' he said. But Hugh-ap-Lloyd
spoke one last time to his liege lord. 'Suffer me yet one more
trial, and you shall see what you shall see.' So Ifan Ddu
suffered him. And Hugh-ap-Lloyd took a christen child from
among the prisoners and laid him on the very stone of offering in the last citadel and offered him with the stone knife
from the Druid grove. And the god of the mountain stream
woke and shouted in his waking to the god of the lake. And
in joy and in power the god of the lake called to the lord of
the storm, and they three turned and rent the invader so that
in the morning no place was found for him." ' He stopped
reading. 'Yes, indeed, Mr Treloar, it is a matter to be treated
with the utmost seriousness.'

'A christen child?' said Septimus.

'It could be a Christian man – the word is very similar to
that for servant or slave. But it is certainly talking about
human sacrifice.'

'I suppose that is why he used the stone knife instead of
the "sword of the new faith"?' Septimus said.

'Yes. A sacrificial knife. As a matter of fact we supposedly
possess it.' He laughed at Septimus's blank astonishment.
'Yes, really. It really is a stone knife. I'll show it you after
dinner. Of course it isn't old really. I should think it was

made in my great-grandfather's time. He was much given to replicas.'

Septimus left the point. 'That passage,' he said, 'do you think John Wesley Jones would really have been unable to translate it?'

'It's difficult to say. Wesley Jones is no mean scholar. But that published text – it's not a good one. My father allowed it to be done in the nineteen twenties and the translator really was not up to the job. The manuscript is very difficult.'

'And what about the rhyme?' Septimus asked. 'I suppose that is related to the legend?'

'Oh, without a doubt. The old myths often exist on two levels, what you might call the literary and the popular. Think of Gawain – he exists in high poetry and the crudest of popular ballads.'

Septimus was prepared to take this information on trust since it was way beyond his scholarship.

'But Shechem would only know the popular version, wouldn't he?'

'Oh, no! No, indeed. Shechem knows all about it.'

'But how?' asked Septimus. 'I doubt if he can even read. Don't tell me he's a scholar as well as Wesley Jones.'

'I fear he knows because I told him,' said Caradoc Lloyd. 'You know the story of the family? Well ever since he could walk Shechem has been about the Plas. He does odd jobs for me, you know. And – well – I am a lonely man, and Shechem liked stories. I suppose he knows as much of the contents of the Red Book as anyone.' He poured port for himself and passed the decanter back to Septimus, but Septimus did not notice. If Shechem knew the contents of the Red Book . . .

'Is he violent?' he asked.

'Shechem is . . . well, like most very powerful men, he is normally very gentle, but it is the gentleness of nature, not of self-control. Do you know Steinbeck's *Of Mice and Men*, Mr Treloar?'

'Yes, I do,' Septimus replied. 'He's like that?'

'Yes. He is like nature itself. I once caught him beating a boy for stoning an injured rabbit. He nearly killed him. He would have killed him, and there was nothing I could do to stop him. Fortunately his mother arrived in time.'

The clock on the mantelpiece chimed. It was a quarter past eight. Hastily Septimus explained about his phone call, apologizing for the cavalier way he seemed to be abusing Caradoc Lloyd's hospitality. Caradoc took up a lamp and led the way back into the little study. He left Septimus with the telephone and a cup of coffee.

Harvey Shortcross was as abrupt as ever, but Septimus, from long years of working with the surgeon, could tell that he was glad to hear his voice. 'Sorry I couldn't ring at lunchtime. Been opening up the living and the dead. Busy day. And what can I do for you?'

If it had been difficult to explain to Caradoc Lloyd, it was nearly impossible over the telephone, and Harvey Shortcross was notorious both for a quick mind and a quick temper. The irascibility soon showed itself.

'My dear man, I always knew you were a fool. But even you cannot expect a surgeon to make a psychiatric diagnosis over a telephone on a patient he has never seen. I would not accept that farago of misused technical terms and old women's tales to make a diagnosis of a crop-bound hen.'

Septimus held the telephone away from his ear as this was going on. He knew the surgeon too well to be daunted but did not see why he should be deafened. 'Yes, I know I'm a fool, Harvey,' he replied patiently. 'You've been telling me so, off and on, for the last quarter-century. But I don't want a diagnosis, only your opinion as to how dangerous such a man could be. You may be a surgeon and not a psychiatrist, but you're a *police* surgeon. Might he really kill someone? But what I really want is for you to pull the strings so that I can talk to the specialist who treated Wesley Jones in that mental hospital. I can't do it officially, because I'm a country parson and not a copper.'

As always, Harvey was to the point. 'Provided your information is accurate, it sounds as if the man was suffering from paranoid delusions when they took him into care. And I'm not surprised. You inundate my home and drown my daughter, and I'll come up with some paranoid delusions myself — persecute the Thames Conservancy.

'Yes, I will put the unofficial wheels in motion. I happen to know the head physician of that hospital. It's all damned irregular and unprofessional, but I'll do it for old times' sake and since you say it's urgent. But if I get struck off the medical register I shall come and haunt you. And you take care of yourself, my lad. I shouldn't enjoy performing an autopsy on you.' He rang off, and Septimus put the phone down. Knowing Harvey as he did, he felt not a little flattered by the last two sentences. Caradoc Lloyd came abruptly into the room. 'It's a most extraordinary thing,' he said, his normal calm courtesy obviously badly shaken.

'What's happened?' Septimus asked.

'The stone knife I was telling you about, the replica. We keep it on the landing. While you were phoning I went to get it — but it's gone.'

11

Choice in the Night

Septimus arrived back at the Mill after a hair-raising drive
through the storm which — as he had guessed it would — had
blown up again with the coming of night. He had parted
from Caradoc Lloyd with scant courtesy and roared out of
the gate while his host was still talking of getting a lantern.
The wind had slammed fitfully at the side of the vehicle as he
had slithered along the track by the lake. He had nearly
piled up twice on the precipitous hairpins, but had managed
somehow to wrench the Land-Rover back on to the road. He
had hurtled along the brief civilization of the main road, his
foot flat on the floorboards, willing the vehicle to travel even
faster, and with a total disregard for the law. If the stone
knife had gone, the chances were that Shechem had got it.
He had access to the Plas, and certainly he would make no
distinction between a replica and the real thing. And he had
last seen Shechem going back into the hills. And little Gwyn
had been out on the lake with John Wesley Jones.

The Land-Rover skidded along the wet lane as he slammed
on the brakes. He left it where it stopped, not bothering about
parking, and ran for the kitchen door. There was a council of
war in progress in the kitchen. Sandy, in anorak, was leaning
on the table. Gwillym Parry was putting on his coat, May
was standing by the sink weeping, a handkerchief to her eyes.

'Ah!' said Sandy. 'Glad you're back, Septimus. Didn't
expect you till later.'

108

'What's up?' Septimus asked, looking at the three stricken figures, guessing the answer.

'It's Gwyn and John Wesley Jones,' said Sandy. 'They went fishing while we went into Portmadoc. We got home half an hour ago, but they're not back.'

'Oh God!' Septimus thought. 'God forgive me. I ought to have known. I ought to have done something.' What he said was, 'Well, we'd better go and find out what's happened.'

The habit of taking charge, of telling stricken people what to do, was so ingrained that it never occurred to him that he was acting in an authoritarian fashion. 'Sandy,' he asked, 'can you row with that timber leg?'

'Of course.'

'Right. Take May in the dinghy across the lake. Look for the boat as you go. Do it on a series of diagonals – don't just row straight across. If you don't find anything, search the shore in both directions. You'll need torches – the bigger the better. Don't go up the mountainside. Gwillym and I will cover that. O.K.?'

'Yes,' said Sandy. He took May's arm and limped from the kitchen. He had lived all his adult life in a disciplined service and knew when argument and question were not necessary.

'Gwillym,' said Septimus, 'have you got a torch?'

'Not with me,' said the Welshman, 'got one at home, though.'

'Right,' said Septimus. 'Come on!' He led the way to the Land-Rover at a run. He was so possessed with a sense of urgency that he did not notice the rain. While Gwillym crossed the road to the Royal Stores Septimus checked that the heavy, rubber-cased flashlight was by the driver's seat and almost unconsciously – he had done it so often in the past – his hand went to his breast pocket to ensure that the pencil torch was in its place by his fountain pen. Septimus started the engine and as he drew level with the shop Gwillym came running out, leaving the door blowing in the wind – something he had not done in twenty years. Septimus went storming along through the night, aware that he had communicated his sense of urgency to the others. He wondered whether to tell Gwillym what he suspected, but rejected the idea. Shechem or Wesley Jones? He was not entirely sure what he did suspect, and anyway the absence of Gwyn and Wesley Jones was susceptible to half a dozen rational explanations: a minor injury, an accident to the boat, loss of an oar. And yet . . . he had had the feeling before and had come to trust it.

He came to the sharp turn at the head of the lake where the tarmac petered out altogether. He went into the corner too fast, and the vehicle with its short wheelbase slid on the mud, headlights making a crazy pattern across rock and wet bracken.

'Watch it!' said Gwillym with admirable aplomb. 'What's the tearing hurry?'

'Just a hunch,' Septimus replied. 'When we arrive I want you to search the quarry and up the Afon. I'll go along the cliff face.' Hugh-ap-Lloyd's cave was in his mind, and his instinct told him that he would find the final answer somewhere along the scree path. It was as if he could see the white face of Shechem's mother in the indistinct cone of the headlights. 'The future is what shall be . . . not even the very wise can see all the future.'

He halted the Land-Rover outside the Maenofferen chapel. The engine sighed into silence and there was only the sound of the wind.

Admirably taciturn, Gwillym tumbled out of the vehicle and set off up the incline, the white beam of his torch flashing from side to side, illuminating wet slate and wet grass. There was a tiny rainbow round the lens of the torch, and as he walked he was calling, 'Gwyn! . . . Gwyn! . . . John! . . .' Septimus followed, his torch also going from side to side. After a few yards the paths diverged and Gwillym's shouting faded on the wind.

Despite the storm, Septimus found the going a good deal

easier with the powerful torch to light the path. He came down through the trees which were roaring in the wind, flashing the bright beam of the torch into the scanty undergrowth around the tree trunks. Despite the turmoil overhead, it was curiously still in the grove, the tree trunks moving hardly at all. It was like a fossilized forest deep beneath a stormy ocean.

He came out into the open again on to the scree path. It seemed almost light after the blackness beneath the trees. He could hear May calling somewhere below him, 'Gwyn! Gwyn bach!' His heart went out to her. He set off along the scree path with a curious premonition that he was going to a foreordained meeting. It was a feeling he had never had before in the many moments of danger and stress he had faced. A feeling almost of well-being, as if after all the years he was about to go and do what he had been born to accomplish. A phrase of Scripture came into his mind. 'Him that overcometh, I will give him a white stone, and in the stone a new name written which no man knoweth save he that receiveth it.' He smiled, wiping the rain from his eyebrows. That was John the Divine on Patmos nineteen hundred years ago, and he was Septimus Treloar on the side of the Moelwyns in the twentieth century. But certainly, like John, he found himself at peace.

He came to the little ravine and climbed it and looked over the top.

There was nothing. He flashed the torch into the cave mouth, but there was no movement. He came out of the ravine and moved on down the path past the cave mouth and along beneath the towering cliffs. He walked for perhaps a mile. He came round an out-thrust spur and there in front of him was a light. He smiled grimly. It was as if he had expected to find the light just there.

It was a hurricane lantern standing on a rock, its light sharp as a diamond in that dark and lonely place. Beside it there were two human figures, the larger sitting on a rock nursing the smaller. It was Shechem and Gwyn. Now Septimus could hear the heart-broken sobbing of the child. It came fitfully on the wind and was in Welsh, but he could tell the meaning – '*Dwi eisio mynd adre* . . . I want to go home, I want to go home.'

Shechem was taking no notice of the crying. He was holding the child close to his chest looking back along the path, his tilted head sharp in profile against the glow of the lantern. For a few seconds which seemed an eternity, Septimus waited, knowing he was dealing with madness, with a mind that moved to strange rhythms of its own, knowing that he must not make a false move. He had little experience to guide him. Once he had coaxed a young woman off the roof of a block of flats. That had taken two hours of caution and sweating patience.

'Shechem!' he called as softly as he could against the wind. 'Shechem! It's only me, Septimus Treloar.' He turned the torch on himself and walked slowly along the path. Shechem lurched to his feet, changing his grip on the child, picking up the lantern. Septimus stopped. Shechem turned and ran dangerously along the scree path, the lantern waving wildly and diminishing in size to the accompaniment of screams from Gwyn.

Septimus remembered the way the path ended abruptly where the rocks jutted out into the lake, the steep scramble down to the lake shore, the black hole leading into the mines that riddled the mountain. He waited awhile, the torch still on himself, and when the hurricane lantern disappeared round the curve of the cliffs, he followed at his best speed.

Shechem had stopped again just beyond the curve. He was standing, looking back, the child in one arm, the lantern in the other hand.

Septimus stopped and turned the torch on himself, forcing himself to be still, to wait. All must be done slowly, despite the heart-rending sobbing of the little boy. It took half a minute to say the Lord's Prayer slowly. He said it twice, articulating the words carefully, paying no manner of heed to the meaning. Then he called,

'Shechem! I want to talk to you. Only talk.' He repeated the words and added, 'If you'll let me, I'll come slowly along the path. You can tell me to stop when you want. Can I do that?'

There was no answer.

'Well, I'm going to come now. But if you want me to stop, you've only to say so, and I'll stop at once.' He moved very slowly along the path, watching Shechem with all his attention, the torch on himself. He had no idea how long that nightmare walk along the scree took. It seemed an eternity with the rain beating on his face, and the massive figure in the light of the lantern seen only indistinctly through the glare of his own torch.

Shechem shouted, 'Stop! Don't come any closer.' Septimus stopped abruptly. Relief flooded over him. If Shechem was prepared to talk, he had achieved his first objective, and he was now close enough to talk instead of having to shout, and that made a profound difference.

Keeping the torch on himself, he said, 'Little Gwyn's ever so unhappy.' He tried to sound calm, unconversational, motherly. It was not easy with his heart pounding like an engine and all his nerves at full stretch.

'Listen to him cry. Poor laddie. Poor little lamb. Why don't you comfort him, Shechem? A little boy crying for his mummy like that.'

This was greeted by a flood of Welsh addressed, not to Septimus but to Gwyn. He could guess the meaning – 'Hush, Gwyn bach, hush your crying.' It made no difference, the little boy only sobbed more loudly, '*Dwi eisio mam* . . . I want my mummy.'

'He wants his mam,' said Septimus. 'Listen to the poor little chap. Why don't you let him go home, Shechem?'

No answer.

'Let him go, Shechem. He's so unhappy. You don't want

little Gwyn to be unhappy, because you're kind. You don't want anyone to be unhappy. Think how frightened he is with the dark. He's cold and wet and frightened. Let him go.'

'No.'

'Caradoc Lloyd told me that you are kind to all little frightened things. He told me how you look after the lambs when they've lost their mothers. He told me you don't like to see rabbits hurt, or birds. Are you really a kind person, Shechem?'

'Yes.'

'Then let little Gwyn go home to his mummy.'

The answer came in Welsh, a sing-song infantile chant like something out of a school playground. Septimus knew it only too well.

> *'A white bird and a silver fish,*
> *A black lamb and a white child,*
> *To help on Mother's washing day.'*

Shechem turned and started to move away. Septimus called after him desperately, 'Wait, Shechem! Wait! Caradoc Lloyd told me something about the white child that I think you ought to know.' Shechem did not stop.

Septimus shouted, 'It won't work, Shechem. It won't work, not unless you know what Caradoc Lloyd told me.'

Shechem stopped and turned back. For one crazy moment Septimus considered making a dive for him. He put the idea aside. It would be quite useless. Shechem was twice as strong as he was, and even if the three of them were not killed in rolling down the precipitous scree, sudden violence would merely spur him into the hideous action that his warped mind had planned. No. The other way was better.

'Shechem,' he said softly, 'Shechem. I was talking to Caradoc Lloyd about the white child. The story's in the Red Book, isn't it, and Caradoc Lloyd told it to you, didn't he?'

'Yes.'

'Well, he told me something about the white child that he

never told you. And it's very important if the charm is going to work and the valley be saved. You want to save the valley, don't you?'

'Yes.' Shechem was quite motionless, lantern in one hand, the sobbing child held firmly in the other arm.

'Caradoc Lloyd knows all the rhymes and all the stories, doesn't he?'

'Yes.'

'Do you want to know what he told me?'

'Yes.' The reply was that of a petulant child, interested despite itself.

Septimus thought to himself, 'Here we go.' He was so concentrating on the minefield of a conversation that he never gave a thought to the possible consequences to himself of what he proposed to do.

'Caradoc Lloyd told me that the rhyme was not really talking about a child at all. Not about a little boy. You know it's all old words in the Red Book, isn't it? And Caradoc Lloyd said the word really means a man with white hair like mine. Shechem, if you use Gwyn the charm won't work. You need a man. That was what Caradoc Lloyd said. And he knows the old stories better than anyone.'

The nightmare conversation by the unearthly light of torch and lantern seemed to take hours while the storm raged around the three of them. Shechem produced childish objections which had the basic logic of the nursery. Septimus produced equally logical counter arguments as if he were some elderly nanny of monumental patience. Gwyn helped, albeit unconsciously, with his abandoned sobbing, '*Dwi eisio mam . . . dwi eisio mam . . .* I want my mummy.'

At last Shechem agreed. For Septimus the relief was like a shaft of sunlight in the middle of the storm, but it did not last long. Shechem involved in an argument about the nature of historical evidence might be like a petulant child. Shechem dealing with the practical matters of movement on the hills, of safety and danger, was another matter altogether. His experience might be with sheep and lambs, the dangers of crag and bog, of ravens and hill foxes, but – as Septimus quickly realized – he now faced very considerable danger himself. The transition was apparent in Shechem's words of agreement.

'You instead of Gwyn, Mr Treloar. Very well. Now. Come very slowly along the path, keeping the torch on yourself. No . . . put it in your other hand. When you are past me I will let little Gwyn go to his mam. Do not try to trick me. I have the knife and I am very strong.'

Septimus did not need reminding of the strength. He knew that Shechem could break him like a doll, and he could see the knife by the light of the lantern. It must be Caradoc Lloyd's replica, a wicked affair a foot long, with a heavy, curved blade.

Septimus moved slowly along the path, the torch on his body. Shechem scrambled up among the rocks above the path, Gwyn still clutched to him. Septimus passed five feet below, and stopped, and turned. Shechem came slowly down to the path, watching the other man all the time. Stooping he put the little boy on the path and let him go. Gwyn ran desperately, his arms stretched out, his little feet stumbling on the rough path. Septimus knelt, still keeping the torch on himself, his free arm outstretched to welcome and embrace the child.

'Oh, Uncle Septimus *bach* . . . Uncle Septimus, take me home, please take me home.' He clung desperately, his arms as far round Septimus's neck as they would go. For a while Septimus said nothing, hugging the child to himself, trying to convey peace and courage.

'Yes. Of course you can go home, Gwyn *bach*.'

'*Dowch, dowch* . . . Come on, then. Let's go.' Gwyn released himself from the encircling arm and tugged, his hand tight round Septimus's index finger. The desperate weeping had subsided into an occasional chest-wracking sob.

'No, I can't come with you, *cariad*. I have to stay with

Shechem. One or other of us has to stay. And Mummy and Daddy are back down the path looking for you. And Uncle John, and Colonel Sandy. They're all so worried. Gwyn . . . do you think you can be a brave boy, ever such a brave boy?' Septimus was desperate. He had to persuade the child.

Gwyn sniffed, his chest still heaving. He looked fearfully at Shechem and then buried his head in Septimus's coat. 'Yes,' he whispered.

'Good! That's my lad. That's my brave Gwyn. Now this is what I want you to do. You take my big torch . . .' He put the torch into the child's two hands. 'See how bright the beam is. Shine it on Shechem. That's it. Now on the big rock there. And this is how you turn it on and off. You press this little button, see? No, you'll have to press it harder than that. That's it! On . . . and off. That's Colonel Sandy's torch out of the Land-Rover.' Gwyn began to forget his terror a little in the wonder and difficulty of managing the torch.

'Now shine it on the path in front of you. That's it. Look how it lights up the stones where you are going to put your feet. Isn't it bright?'

'*O ydi mae* . . . Yes, it does,' said Gwyn, his terrors lost in the delight of it.

'Now this is what I want my brave boy to do. Keep hold of the torch with both hands. Yes . . . like that. I want you to go along the path. You know the path don't you?'

Yes. Gwyn knew the path. He had been along it with Uncle John and they had looked into the black hole that led into the mountain.

'Good. Well, you go back along the path – all the way you have come with Uncle John. You go through the wood, taking ever such care not to trip over the roots. Remember how I tripped over and fell in a bramble? Then you go down the track and you'll find Colonel Sandy's motor just by the old chapel. You know where I mean?'

'Yes.'

'You'll find Mummy there. I promise. Or if she's not

there, she'll come soon. Do you think you can do that – on your own – like a brave chap?'

'*Ydw* . . . Yes . . .' doubtfully, and then more brightly, 'if you come with me.'

'I can't come yet. I'll come later. If Mummy's not there when you get to the motor, you're not to go looking for her because she'll come very soon. She's looking for you and you might miss each other in the dark. You're to climb into the motor and wait. There's a blanket in the back. You wrap yourself up to get warm again and sit in the driver's seat. Mummy or Daddy or Uncle John or Colonel Sandy will come back to the motor soon. I promise. And they'll find you there. And if you want to, you can blow the horn. Do you think you can do all that?'

'Yes. If you come with me.'

It took several minutes to persuade the little boy to venture into the dark on his own. Perhaps it was sheer desperation, perhaps it was the shivering cold, or fear of Shechem, or Septimus's calm certainty that he could do it – whatever it was, at last he steeled himself to the journey and set off at a stumbling trot down the path.

'Don't run,' Septimus called after him. 'Don't run, Gwyn *bach*. In case you have a fall. And give my love to Mummy and the others.'

The flickering beam of the torch vanished round the corner and the slight noise of the little boy's feet faded in the storm.

Septimus stood up from where he had been kneeling on the path, automatically dusting his knees. He did not notice that it made not the slightest difference since his trousers were soaked.

'Come,' said Shechem. 'Let us go, Mr Treloar.' Nothing could have sounded more sane, but Septimus knew that nothing could have been more dangerous.

12

Under the Mountain

Septimus moved slowly along the scree path. It was difficult
to see where he was putting his feet because Shechem was
coming behind him with the lantern. He was also terribly
conscious of the stone knife which Shechem was carrying in
his other hand. When he had been talking with little Gwyn
he had heard but not really registered where Shechem was
intending to go. It was only now that the full horror of it
came upon him. 'The black hole' – that was what Gwyn had
called it. To go through that horrible, dripping place, down
and down into the bowels of the mountain. Miles of labyrin-
thine tunnels, the bitter cold, the dripping of water, rock falls,
and the black flood water rising level by level as the cold gods
of the underworld took back their own from the puny invasion
of men. And there would be the awful blackness! One hurricane lantern and two men in the dark heart of the mountain
under all those millions and millions of tons of rock. For a
while he was seized by a terror such as perhaps only children
and animals feel, a blind, unreasoning terror of some unimaginable horror. He would turn and fight Shechem. He
would hurl himself from the path and down the scree, let
his body be broken on the rocks – at least it would be in the
blessed open air instead of down that appalling hole. He was
on the very point of jumping, he had indeed tensed his body
for the spring when two things came to his aid. The first was
his police training, the second his faith. He suddenly realized

that if he jumped Shechem could go back for Gwyn, and it would all have been useless. Gwyn would still die. On the heels of the practical consideration came a verse from the Psalms, a verse which he had read that morning as he had said matins with scant attention.

'Whither shall I go from thy Spirit? If I climb up into heaven thou art there. If I go down into hell, thou art there also.' A man had to die sometime, and he was aware that he was well over halfway on the Biblical obstacle race of 'three-score years and ten'. And at least his death would serve a purpose. Gwyn would live. A death like that, however unpleasant in its details, was a good deal more than most people got. Better a last fight with Shechem, even if it was a hopeless fight in that black pit, than doddering mindlessness, or death by surgery in some anonymous hospital bed.

So his faith came to his aid, not by taking away his terror, but by making it possible to think again, to control terror. He ceased to be like the animal or the child, and started to think, and his training came to his aid. He had faced danger before, and saved his own life and the lives of others by self-control, by observation, by waiting for the right moment to perform the right action. He surveyed possibilities. He was a powerful man, but a child in comparison with Shechem. Very well. It would have to be cunning and not brute force. But Shechem was cunning – with the cunning of an animal on the mountains. Very well, again. He, Septimus, was not a fox or a raven, he was a man, and he would oppose animal cunning with the cunning of a man, with the knowledge gained from long experience of physical violence. He wasn't dead yet. Not by a long chalk. And he would play the business out to the bitter end.

Talk! That was the first thing.

'Shechem!' he called over his shoulder, 'that knife you've got. It belongs to Caradoc Lloyd?'

'Yes.'

'Shechem! You stole it!' Septimus tried to sound shocked,

like an infant school teacher investigating a theft of chewing gum. 'You stole it from Caradoc Lloyd who has been so kind to you.'

'I needed it.'

'Caradoc Lloyd told me something about that knife, Shechem.'

No answer.

'Don't you want to know what Caradoc Lloyd told me?'

'What did he tell you?'

'He told me at dinner tonight. He said it wasn't an old knife at all. He said his great-grandfather had it made because he liked making copies of old things. Just as you like making things for the tourists. It isn't Hugh-ap-Lloyd's knife at all.'

'Shut up!' said Shechem with sudden violence. 'You talk too much, Mr Treloar. The knife will do for what I want. Shut up or I'll hit you.' Septimus said no more. He reflected grimly that he might have managed to talk Gwyn out of Shechem's hands, but it did not look as if he was going to be able to do the same for himself.

They came to the entrance to the mine shaft.

'Stop,' said Shechem.

Obediently Septimus came to a halt and turned, his nerves tense, hoping he would find Shechem sufficiently close for a sudden attack to have some possibility of success. If he could not fight Shechem at least he was heavy enough, given surprise, to knock him bodily from the scree path.

But Shechem had stopped a full ten feet behind him, and was holding up the lantern so that most of its light fell on Septimus. If you had experience in dealing with cornered and savage animals, Septimus thought bitterly, you learned to keep your distance.

Shechem came cautiously forward and pointed with his free hand to the black hole. 'Climb in,' he said.

Septimus tried another tack.

'No,' he said firmly, trying to sound as matter-of-fact as

possible. 'No. I won't go into that ridiculous hole for you or anyone else.'

For a moment Shechem was nonplussed. 'But you promised.' His voice was suddenly that of a child.

Ever afterwards Septimus reckoned that if he had played the right card at that moment, the whole horrible business would have ended then and there. Sadly, neither afterwards nor in the stress of the moment, could he work out what the right card was. He tried to meet Shechem on his own infantile level.

'I'm tired of this game, Shechem. I'm wet and I'm cold, and I bet you are. I want to go home like Gwyn. Let's call it off and play another time when it isn't raining.' He moved purposefully towards the other man. Shechem thrust out a hand and pushed Septimus on the chest so that he stumbled backwards and fell on the path.

'I told you to shut up,' he said. 'Get in there, or I'll throw you in.' Septimus struggled to his feet, his knees bruised, the palm of his left hand bleeding. He moved to the hole, but shaken by the fall, he was seized again by terror of the darkness and the unknown.

'I can't,' he said desperately. 'I've no idea what distance I shall fall inside.'

'It is not far,' said Shechem. 'And the floor of the shaft is flat.' Septimus still hesitated.

'You'd better walk, Mr Treloar. Or I shall knock you out and carry you.'

The practical point penetrated Septimus's fear. Conscious, he had hope of life, unconscious, he had none at all.

Septimus scrambled up on to the barricade of loose stone and let himself down carefully into the darkness. The difference was so extraordinary that his terror vanished in his curiosity and his habit of observation. The noise of the storm sounded so different. Suddenly it was distant, as if a thick curtain had dropped, or as if one had moved inside an organ while it was being played.

He dropped to his knees, aware that he had a few seconds before Shechem joined him inside. He swept the rock floor with his hands, searching for a piece of iron, for a stone, for anything that he could use as a weapon.

There was nothing. The floor was like rough concrete, and on its surface there were only pebbles. The light of the storm lantern grew bright over his head, and Shechem's voice came, hollow, echoing away and away into the depths of the mine.

'Stand up and turn round.'

Septimus did as he was told.

Shechem had placed the lantern on top of the breastwork which had been built across the hole. Septimus could see the indistinct oval of his face, his hair blowing in the storm.

'Now move back . . . slowly. Further than that . . . Further. Now turn with your face to the wall. Now kneel down.' There was certainly no chance of attacking Shechem as he climbed through the hole.

'Now get up and walk down the tunnel,' said Shechem. Septimus obeyed. He had heard nothing of Shechem climbing through the hole.

He walked deliberately into the blackness, troubled as he had been on the path outside by the fact that he could not see where he was putting his feet. He tried to quell his horror of some unseen hole in front of his feet with the rational knowledge that Shechem knew what he was doing. It was true enough, but not much comfort in that cold and echoing place where he could see only his own shadow sloping away into darkness.

The tunnel led steadily downward, and despite the echoing of their feet, it was quiet after the clamour of the storm outside. Septimus knew that once they stopped moving the silence would be the silence of the tomb. He swerved away from the word and set himself to observe.

The drip of water which had first horrified him about the tunnel ceased after the first twenty yards. It must be surface water, rain running down the mountain, penetrating hardly

123

at all into the rock of which the mountain was made. He noted that he was not suffering from the claustrophobia he had expected. The tunnel was shaped like a flying buttress: one wall nearly vertical, the roof and the second wall joined in a gentle curve. He could see by the light of the lantern that it was not slate. It was solid rock, presumably granite, solid and secure enough to support anything.

Down they went in silence, apart from the echoing of their footsteps. Septimus started to count paces. If he were ever to escape from this underground maze, he simply must learn something of its geography. He tried to divide his attention, one part to count, the other part to observe and consider possibilities of escape. They passed various tunnels branching off to right and left, but Septimus ignored them. They were clearly minor affairs, and it was going to be quite difficult enough keeping the main route in mind. '673 . . . 674 . . . 675 . . .' He hoped it wasn't 775.

There was something different about the tunnel ahead. The roof was getting higher and the shadows had changed. A few paces later they came at right angles into a much larger tunnel. It curved away in either direction, climbing to the right. In the middle of it were the rusting remains of a narrow-gauge railway line. Septimus stopped, unsure what he was supposed to do.

'Turn left,' Shechem ordered, and then he added conversationally, 'We've come down an adit. They used it for drainage when the pumps were working. This used to be the main way out of the mine, but it's blocked both ends by falls.'

'Eight hundred and three and turn left on to the railway,' said Septimus to himself. Later he would have to reverse the directions – if there ever were a later. But that could wait. Learning the way down was difficult enough.

The second tunnel was clearly much less stable than the first. Septimus was no geologist, but he guessed that the first tunnel had followed the natural line of the rock, whereas this one had been cut regardless of the lie of the mountain, taking the shortest route to a slate seam. The surface of the walls varied as they passed through different strata. There were places where it was supported with great hoops of rusting steel like the mouldering rib cage of a dinosaur. There were piles of rock across the tramway where there had been minor falls from the roof. Septimus guessed that the tunnel was in an extremely dangerous condition and no one but a madman would enter it. But there was nothing he could do about that.

Now there were more holes on either side and Septimus had brief glimpses into vast caverns, the light of the lantern glancing from dull walls of slate. He guessed that these were the 'chambers' from which the slate was taken. Chamber after chamber, forty, sixty feet high, leaving a thick pillar of slate to support the terrible weight of the mountain, until the width of the slate seam had been gutted; then down a level, leaving a thick floor, and chamber after chamber, and each pillar exactly beneath the one above; chambers and levels, men burrowing like ants for half a century, and the whole honeycombed structure depending upon accuracy and the skill of the miners; a mountain like a beehive, its stability depending on the fact that men had got their sums right.

'232 . . . 233 . . . 234 . . .' There was a noise ahead, a murmur, growing quickly into a roar, as if there were a football match at the end of the tunnel and a goal had been scored. At 453 the dampness of the air told him what it was. An underground stream was cataracting into the depths below. Just before the unseen fall they turned left into a slate cavern. Septimus reversed his calculations in his head to see if he could remember them.

'Slate cavern. Turn right by waterfall. 453 paces along tramway. Watch out for rock falls. Turn right into adit shaped like quarter oval.' He need not remember how many paces led to the blessed open air, to the storm in the night which seemed so welcome.

Now they were going down so steeply that Septimus had to turn and move backwards, using his hands. Shechem, in front of him now, did not need to turn. With the agility of the years spent on the precipitous mountains, he moved easily, leaning far back, the lantern steady in his hand. The slope could not have been far off forty-five degrees. They were still following the rusty rails of the tramway. They had branched at a point from the main line in the tunnel that led to the waterfall. Septimus guessed that they must be descending one of the underground inclines. Presumably there had once been a winch and a rope to haul the slate blocks up from the depths. What was it Gwillym had said? Three hundred feet below sea level and it takes a day to get a slate block out? Something like that.

They came to the bottom of the incline, and Septimus's right hand which was clutching one of the rusty rails brushed against something hard and angular, something which rolled as the back of his hand touched it. He let go of the rail and felt about in the darkness. He felt first the spike holding the rail, then the rotting sleeper to which it was fixed, then pieces of slate debris, then . . . there it was. He gripped it, sliding his fingers along it, trying to analyse what it was without looking at it. It was a heavy coach-bolt. It was about six inches long, and the square nut and the washers were still in place. He closed his palm on it and turned his right side away from the light of the lantern. Obedient to Shechem's order he waited at the bottom of the incline.

They crossed the smooth floor of the cavern, went through a narrow entrance, and came into a second cavern. They passed through three more, the lantern throwing weird shadows across vaulted slate and massive pillars. It was like the crypt of some unimaginable vast medieval cathedral.

'This is Level Seven,' said Shechem, suddenly conversational again, his voice echoing under the mountain, '. . . even . . . even . . . even.' 'We have to go up again to Level Six.'

'Why?' asked Septimus. It would be something gained if he could get Shechem to talk.

'Because of the falls and the main tunnel being blocked.'

'So –' Septimus began, but Shechem cut him off.

'Now turn right. And shut up.'

They came to the foot of another incline, this one leading up again, out of the cavern. It was as steep as the one they had descended and a good deal longer. Needing both hands to haul himself upward, Septimus slipped the coach-bolt into his pocket, turning his body sideways so that the action would not be visible to Shechem. When he reached the top of the incline he was trembling from the sheer physical effort of the climb. His chest heaving, he turned back to look at Shechem. Even Shechem was having to use a hand to help himself. He was leaning forward, holding the lantern and the knife in one hand, grasping the tramway rail with the other.

Now, Septimus thought, now was the moment to attack, while Shechem was powerless on the last few feet of the steep slope. He tensed, his hand closing over the bolt in his pocket. Then he relaxed. If he threw himself bodily at Shechem, the lantern would certainly be smashed and . . . it simply would not do. They would both roll down that precipitous incline even if they did not fall off it, and both eventualities would be equally lethal. The moment, when it came – if it came – must be the right moment.

They were in another tunnel now, its construction so like the one that led to the waterfall that Septimus guessed it must be the same one. He asked Shechem, and it was the same tunnel. They had passed the rockfall by descending to the lower level and coming up again. They moved onward a further 170 paces, and now they came to a new obstacle. The tunnel ended without warning on the edge of a precipice. How deep it was Septimus had no means of knowing. Once there had been a bridge over it, for the tramway lines jutted out into the darkness over the chasm, bending under their own weight and disappearing from sight before – presumably – they came to an end. All that remained of the bridge was a tangle of collapsed girders hanging over the edge and a single massive beam about nine inches wide. It was butted solidly into the rock and like the rails it disappeared into the darkness, but unlike the rails it was still horizontal. Presumably it was still attached to the other side of the chasm. The thought of crossing it brought back all Septimus's terror. To shuffle out on that! Over that crack in the mountain of unknown depth, the light behind him, unable to see where he was putting his feet . . . he could not do it. He simply could not do it. He was about to turn and refuse, to stand and fight, when he realized that this was the moment he had been waiting for since he had first climbed into the mine. Once he was across and Shechem was on the beam, he would be master, especially with the coach-bolt that he had in his pocket. The inequality of their strength would mean nothing at all. All the advantages would be his. As he turned he forgot his terrors and drew breath to ask if he had to cross. As he did so Shechem hit him, hard on the side of the jaw. Septimus was flung sideways against the tunnel wall. He slithered to the floor and lay still.

I3

The Cave of the Stone of Offering

Septimus groaned as he came back to consciousness. At first he was aware only of the pain in his jaw, and could not remember what had happened or where he was. He opened his eyes. There was a lantern standing on a flat rock a few feet from his head. Just a lantern — nothing else, all the rest was darkness. How could there be a lantern on a rock and nothing else? It was a hurricane lantern. Memory came flooding back and he realized that Shechem must have knocked him out and carried him over the beam which spanned the chasm. Like Septimus he must have foreseen the opportunities of escape that the bridge offered, and had taken the most direct way out of the difficulty. As Septimus reached this rather grim conclusion Shechem came into his line of vision, his silhouette enormous against the glow of the lantern. He was carrying a pile of wood which he dropped on the rock. He picked up the lantern and came over to Septimus.

'I'm very sorry I had to do that, Mr Treloar, to hit you. But it was the only safe way to get you across the bridge.' The apology sounded quite sane and sincere – Shechem was really sorry. Septimus had a hysterical desire to giggle which took some quelling. If you proposed to stick a stone knife into an acquaintance and burn his lifeless corpse on a stone altar several hundred feet underground, it seemed a little otiose to apologize for clipping him on the jaw first.

'I'm sorry as well,' he said, being as matter-of-fact as he could manage.

He struggled to his feet, feeling his jaw tenderly. 'Where are we now?'

Shechem pointed to the rock where he had laid the wood. '*Carreg yr offrwm,*' he said, 'the cave of the stone of offering.' He came closer. 'I must tie your hands, Mr Treloar.'

'In a minute,' said Septimus. 'But tell me something first, Shechem. Why are you doing this? First the bird and then the fish, then the black lamb of the white ewe, and now . . . me. Why are you doing it?'

He knew the answers, but he desperately wanted to gain time for his head to clear. There was not much more time, and the right moment had not yet appeared. Perhaps this was it. He knew dimly what he was going to do when Shechem came close to tie his hands. But he must, he simply must clear the cobwebs from his brain if he was to have any chance of success.

'Because it is what Hugh-ap-Lloyd did,' said Shechem.

'He cleansed the valley and so will I.' Even in that desperate extremity Septimus could recognize the dignity in his voice.

'*Dyna'r unig ffordd*,' he continued, his voice echoing in the open spaces of the cavern with nothing childish about it. 'It is the only way. They come with their tools and their machines as they have come to other valleys. They will flood this valley as they have flooded other valleys. They will blast the rocks and build roads. They will drive the goats from the high places of the mountain and the raven from her nest until all the peace of the wilderness is gone. *Dyna'r unig ffordd*. To call upon the old gods. That is the only way.'

Septimus's head was clearer now.

'Do you think the old gods will answer?'

'Yes. They answered before when Hugh-ap-Lloyd called on them.'

'How do you know? Perhaps it is only a story. A story Caradoc Lloyd told you when you were a little boy.'

'I know because it is in Caradoc Lloyd's book. The Red Book which tells what happened.'

'But all stories in books are not true. Some of them are made up. If you kill me and it does not work, you will have killed me for nothing.'

'I should also have killed the others for nothing. But it is in the Red Book so I know it is true.' There was anger in his voice now.

'What others?' Septimus asked.

'The fish and the bird and the lamb. If it is not true I should have killed them without reason. It is wrong to kill without reason.'

Despite all that had happened, it still came as a shock to Septimus to realize that the life or death of a human being could mean no more and no less than the death of an animal.

'If you kill me, they will call it murder, Shechem. They will lock you up, and you will not walk on the mountains for many years, perhaps not ever again.'

'Then I shall die. But it will not matter because the hills

130

and the valleys will be free again. Now we must stop talking, Mr Treloar. Go and stand by the stone with your back to me.' Septimus obeyed, turning his body slightly as he moved so that he could slip the coach-bolt from his pocket. He reached the stone and stood with his hands resting on it. He was concentrating all his attention on what was happening behind him, but even so some tiny part of his mind noted that the stone was a larger replica of Hugh-ap-Lloyd's altar, with the same shape and a similar band of decoration. There was only one difference. It was much bigger. Big enough to take a man. The lantern shadows shifted as Shechem came softly up behind him. Septimus held the coach-bolt loosely, trying to relax the tension in his muscles, watching the shifting shadows. Many things passed through his mind as he waited, for this was his last chance. If he failed, he would assuredly die. The terrors of the last hours fell finally from him. It was him or Shechem now. He was not so arrogant as to suppose that he was worth more in the scheme of things than Shechem was, but certainly he was less of a public menace. And if he failed? Someone else would have to cope with Shechem. And for himself . . . ? It *had* been a good life, and a full one, and on the whole a merry one. He hoped little Gwyn would enjoy life as much as he had. The flickering shadows stopped, and there was the slightest sound of metal grating on stone as Shechem put down the lantern, as he must do, needing two hands for the rope. Septimus had his head down, hoping to see the lantern or Shechem's feet beneath his outstretched arm. But he could see nothing but rock, so he could not judge the distance accurately. But Shechem must be close, closer than he had been since they started the nightmare journey down the mine. His attention must be largely concentrated on the rope.

'Put your hands behind your back,' said Shechem.

'Certainly,' said Septimus as calmly as possible. He raised his hands from the stone and with all the speed and strength he could muster, he swung round to his left, his right arm outstretched, the coach-bolt held loosely in the palm of his hand.

In the split second that he had to adjust his attack he saw that Shechem was standing a little further back than he had hoped. He flung his right foot forward as if he was a fencer making a lunge, his arm at full stretch. It was so well-timed and so sudden that Shechem did not even move. For a fraction of a second Septimus saw him as a great menacing shadow in the light of the lamp, then his right arm came plunging down and the heavy bolt with its cruel edges of nut and washers and domed head hit Shechem just behind the ear. As the blow connected Septimus thought, 'It will kill him, and I'm sorry.'

It was as if Shechem had been struck by a vehicle. The blow knocked him sideways, his feet in the air, and he went crashing across the stone floor taking the hurricane lantern with him. The lantern burst, and in a second there was a spreading pool of flaming paraffin licking across the rock with Shechem weltering in the middle of it, his clothes beginning to flare. Septimus acted almost instantly, but with the intensity of the moment, even as he moved, he was aware of many things. For the first and only time, in the livid glare of the flaming oil he saw the whole cavern, its great arched roof sixty feet above his head, its floor sloping gently like a stone beach to black, motionless water which reflected on its mirror surface the lurid flames. He experienced triumph – his stratagem had succeeded against a man half his age and twice his strength, and he thought viciously, 'Serve him right if he burns. Only what he was going to do to me.' Then he thought, 'Oh God! You poor devil!' and he was unaware that he had cried it aloud, and before Shechem had ceased to roll Septimus had run, and was beating at his clothes, turning him over and over out of the reach of the flames.

He rolled the inert body clear of the fire, gasping with the effort, trembling with exhaustion. So at last he rested, kneeling, his hands flat on the floor, his energy drained.

The oil fire began to die down, the flames lessening, the shadows closing in like wolves around a dying camp fire. Septimus passed a hand across his brow and shook his head like a dog. There was one thing he must do before total darkness overtook him. He turned back to Shechem and felt in his pockets and around his belt. He removed a clasp-knife, but that was not what he was looking for. He moved back towards the stone altar, searching along the line of Shechem's fall. When he got to the altar, his attention was deflected a moment. From the pile of timber on top of the stone he selected a hefty club. Swinging it in his hand he continued his search.

It was on the farthest edge of the circle of fire that he found the stone knife. Surprisingly it was still in one piece, although there was a large chip out of the sharp blade. He looked at the hideous thing and was tempted to throw it into the water, but caution and common sense prevailed. He thrust it into his belt and went back to Shechem.

The fire was small now. It could not last much longer. Another thought struck him, and he shambled to the edge of the silent, black water and knelt on the stone. He had to steel himself to plunge his head in. His reason told him that it was simply water, the same stuff that ran in the streams in the bright mountain world up above. His imagination conjured up many-tentacled monsters lurking in the inky depths below. The water on his face and head was cold, as if it had come off ice. He came up gasping . . . and realized how thirsty he was. He bent forward again and drank and drank, his head down like an animal. He came up for air, his head clearer now. The burns on his hands were smarting with the cold of the water. He knelt a moment, realized what he had to face when the flickering fire died altogether, and bent again, and drank and drank until he could drink no more. He returned once more to the inert body of Shechem and sat on the stone floor and watched the fire die. It shrank from a pool a yard in diameter to a foot, the flames shrinking in height as the perimeter contracted and turning from red to orange to a sickly blue. Now the pool was no bigger than a saucer. He watched it intently, as a man might watch an ant scurrying across a paving slab. It flickered, went out, then flared once again, a last gesture of defiance against the triumphant darkness. Then it went out altogether and there was only the foul smell of paraffin smoke in a blackness that was like velvet over the eyes and a silence that only the stone deaf normally know. Septimus reached out and touched Shechem's coat. It was homely to his touch and he felt a queer burst of affection for this man who had tried to kill him. It was as if he had only two senses left to him, those of smell and touch.

He did not know whether Shechem was dead or alive, and for the moment he felt too numb to find out what horrible damage he had done with the coach-bolt. He could not remember whether he was on Level Six or Level Seven. He could not remember the details of the journey into the mountain, the details he had tried so hard to learn. Evidently the crack on the jaw he had received from Shechem was no sort of aid to memory. He remembered with the utmost vividness the beam across the chasm which he had been facing when Shechem hit him. Even if he knew the route back to the bridge, even if he could remember the route on the other side of the bridge he had no light. He had given Sandy's torch to little Gwyn, and the storm lantern was smashed. For the first time in his life he gave up hope. He had probably killed Shechem, but at least he had saved Gwyn. 'A life for a life,' he thought. But that was Old Testament, not Christian at all. He could not think what the Christian thing was. And he was so tired! 'A life for a life. An eye for an eye. A tooth for a tooth.' That was Moses – and the Chief Constable of the Thames Valley Division of the police. The Chief Constable was an old friend of his and he had once quoted the passage to Septimus as a philosophical basis for police work. To Septimus it had always seemed inadequate.

The thought of the police made him wish that the way to

the surface was impassable. A pity that bridge could not be thrown into the chasm. He did not want old colleagues or earnest young constables – or Gwillym Parry or skilled Welsh miners for that matter – earning posthumous George Crosses in futile attempts at trying to find out what had happened to him. It was better this way. It would be a lot easier for Mrs Shechem. He still did not know what her surname was. He never would now, and it did not matter. Then he thought of his dog, Grace, a Great Dane puppy. Rosemary Barton, the churchwarden's wife, would look after Grace. So thinking, he lay down, unaware that as he did so he had turned up his coat collar, unaware that he was using Shechem's thigh as a pillow. So he slept.

14

The Other One

It was the cold that woke him. He came sharply to consciousness and found that he was shivering. It was a moment before he remembered where he was, then there was a wave of panic, then his mind was alert, beginning to examine possibilities. He did not know how long he had slept, but the sleep – and no doubt the water he had drunk – had done him good. He did not even remember his previous mood of resignation. He found that his mind was much clearer. He was beginning to remember directions as if he were watching someone else do a jigsaw puzzle. The bridge where Shechem had attacked him, the tunnels, the inclines up and down. The distances . . . ? He could not yet remember the figures but perhaps they would come back if he gave them a chance to creep unnoticed into his memory. He must think of something else. He sat up and deliberately opened his eyes, and as he made the decision he realized that he did not know whether they were open or shut. He flicked them up and down experimentally. It was difficult to tell whether they were open or shut because the position made no manner of difference and he could only tell by the feel of the muscles, and he had never had to do that before. It must be like this to be stone blind. What should he think of? Shechem!

Where was Shechem? He had entirely forgotten that he had used him as a pillow. He felt around him in the blackness and was surprised and relieved when his hand came into contact with cloth. It took a moment to identify the cloth by touch alone. It was corduroy. He could tell by the ridges under his fingertips. His hand must be on Shechem's calf. He moved it up the slope of cloth. No, it was Shechem's thigh for he could feel the coat against the back of his hand. He moved on and upward, exploring with both hands now. He found shirt and shirt buttons, and slid his hand inside feeling for the heart across a mat of hair. He could feel no movement. But that was hardly surprising through all that hair and muscle. You might as well try to detect a central-heating boiler under coconut matting on a concrete floor. By working down from the shoulder he eventually found Shechem's pulse. It was slow but steady. He was grateful that Shechem was still alive though he could not tell how hurt he was.

He remembered the water. That was what Shechem needed. But in which direction was it? The cave floor sloped to it, but in this darkness you could not detect the slope. How could he do anything without a light?

He should have thought of his pencil torch before, but it was only now that he remembered it. And remembering it, he could hardly bear to feel for it. Suppose it had dropped out in the fight? Suppose the bulb was smashed? At length he reached into his jacket pocket. His fountain pen, his propelling pencil and – yes! there it was. He drew it out and held the smooth cylinder in his hand not daring to press the clip which acted as a switch. He knew with absolute clarity that if it did not work he had reached the end of his personal road. In his mind's eye he could see the bulb of the torch, a tiny thing of glass and metal with a thread of wire in it, perhaps an eighth of an inch long and thinner than a hair. Odd that one's life should depend on such a little thing.

He closed his eyes and pressed the switch.

He opened his eyes. A narrow beam of unbelievably white light was shining on Shechem's face. His eyes were closed and blood was pulsing across his cheek. Septimus switched off the torch, knowing that he must conserve the short life of the tiny batteries. Kneeling there he started to pray, a prayer of pure gratitude. 'Hail Mary, full of grace, the Lord is with thee . . .' It was not an Anglican devotion at all, and certainly not one he normally used, but it was the one that came to his mind. As he said it he was thinking of Shechem's mother and the half-promise he had made to her.

'. . . Holy Mary, Mother of God, pray for us sinners now and at the hour of our death.' He finished the devotion, turned on the torch and swung it in a circle until he caught the gleam of water in the beam.

Using the torch as little as possible, he went to the water and soaked his handkerchief and returned to Shechem. He made the journey several times, sometimes squeezing the water into Shechem's mouth, sometimes using it to bathe the swelling wound on the side of his head.

Shechem rolled over on to his side and muttered something in Welsh. Septimus hutched across on his bottom and took the other man's head in his lap and continued to bathe the wound. It seemed to go on for quite some time. Suddenly, and with an energy which reminded Septimus of the enormous strength in that bulky body, Shechem sat up, casting himself free from Septimus who moved cautiously away in the darkness. If Shechem had really come back to life he could stop being a nurse and had better start being a copper again. He waited.

Shechem spoke in Welsh, paused and then repeated the phrase more loudly; then again, more loudly still, a great cry this time, a shout echoing in the darkness.

Septimus spoke. He tried to sound as banal as possible.

'I do not know what you are shouting. But you are with me, Septimus Treloar, in the cave of the Stone of Offering. You wanted to kill me. But I knocked you out.'

Shechem replied in English. 'Mr Treloar, where are you?'

'I am here close to you in the darkness.'

'Where?'

Septimus forced a laugh, trying to make it sound easy – which only made it sound worse. It was more like a hyena barking than a laugh.

'You want to kill me and you expect me to tell you where I am?'

The reply was childlike and produced with the utmost seriousness.

'I do not want to kill you, Mr Treloar. Why should I want to kill you? It was you who saved little Gwyn's life, and I love little Gwyn.'

Septimus was entirely out of his depth with this lunatic conversation. He had heard of schizophrenia, of the split mind. He had even had some experience of it. But what a clout on the side of the head might do to a schizophrenic he had no idea. Could it work as a crude sort of shock treatment? Or was Shechem being cunning? That was a possibility that made him grip his club more tightly and listen for any sound of movement in the darkness.

'Then why did you take him away from John Wesley Jones if you love him?'

'It wasn't me. It was the other one.'

'What other one?'

'The one that thought that with little Gwyn he could make the bad men go away and not flood the valley.'

'And what happened to this other one?'

There was a long silence. The answer came plaintively. 'I don't know.' There was another pause, and then Shechem asked, 'Where's little Gwyn?'

Septimus felt the hair prickle on his scalp. 'We sent him home,' he said. 'Don't you remember, Shechem? We gave him my big torch.'

'Oh, yes! I remember now. The other one wanted to do bad things. So we sent him home.' He started to hum to himself and then to sing. Septimus recognized the words but not the tune. He had never heard it sung before.

> *'A white bird and a silver fish,*
> *A black lamb and a white child,*
> *To help on Mother's washing day.'*

'Now,' Septimus thought. 'Now we shall see.'

'Mr Treloar,' the voice was plaintive, 'Mr Treloar, I want to be closer to you. It's dark.'

Septimus did not reply at once. He had no real knowledge of what was going on in Shechem's muddled brain. He was aware of the dangers – he had had sufficient demonstration of the man's cunning and strength. Yet if his madness had changed – even temporarily, there was hope that both of them might escape from this tomb alive.

'I don't trust you,' he said brutally. 'For all I care you can stay there in the darkness and rot.'

There was the sound of sobbing, the broken-hearted crying of a child.

'Why? Why? It's dark and I'm lonely, and I'm cold – so cold.'

Septimus thought of shock. Even Shechem's massive constitution must have been shaken by the blow with the coach-bolt. It would have killed most people, and he suddenly realized just how cold he was himself.

'I don't trust you because you tried to kill me.'

'I didn't! I didn't! It was the other.'

Septimus went on ruthlessly. 'Yes, you did. It was you. There is no "other". It was Shechem who killed the trout. It was Shechem who killed the bird. It was Shechem who killed the lamb . . .'

'No! No! Not me. It was the other!'

'It was you who brought me down here. You – Shechem. It was you who was going to kill me on the Offering Stone so that the bad men would go away and leave the valley alone. It was you, Shechem! You! You! You!'

'Not me!' The voice was a snivel now, a child weeping in the dark. 'Not me! It was the other.'

Septimus relaxed a little. He had pressed Shechem as hard as he knew how, and he had still got the same answer. It was 'the other'. Well . . . so long as it remained like that.

'Very well,' he said, gently now, 'you can come to me, Shechem.' In the darkness he raised the club, ready to strike. 'I'll keep talking,' he said, 'and you come towards my voice.' There was a scuffle in the darkness. He tried hard to keep his voice conversational, but it was like being in a dark cage with a wild animal of uncertain temper. 'Shechem, we're both stuck here under the mountain – because the other one put us here. And it's only you that know the way out.' He felt hands on his legs and he wanted to scream. But he did not scream, he babbled on, talking banal nonsense while the hands explored his body and he raised the club above his head. The fumbling hands stopped and the little-boy voice said, 'Please hold my hand, Mr Treloar.'

Septimus groped in the darkness, and fumbled, and took a hand twice the size of his own. A weight descended across Septimus's knees and the little-boy voice said, 'That's better. I feel more comfy now.'

Septimus sat there, Shechem's head on his lap, listening to his breathing. It lengthened and deepened, and as it did, so Septimus let the club fall to his side. He let go of it and brought up his hand and ran it softly over Shechem's shaggy hair. The breathing did not change. Shechem was asleep.

15

Out of the Darkness

Only Shechem knew the way back to the bridge. That, Septimus told himself, was the point. Wandering alone in the tunnels and caverns of the mine was not an inviting prospect. He would certainly try it if he had to, but it would be far better if Shechem's changed mood was still on him when he woke. He closed his mind to the future that would then face Shechem, and to the fact that he himself would have to ensure that future.

Cold and cramped, he had almost fallen asleep again when Shechem stirred and groaned. He felt the weight of Shechem's head lift from his thighs. Alert again, Septimus put his hand on his club and waited.

'Mr Treloar?'

'Yes?' Evidently Shechem had remembered where he was and what had happened.

'Let's get out of here before the other one comes back.' It was impossible to gauge whether Shechem was still reasonably safe or whether he had reverted to his former cunning. Septimus decided he would have to risk it. Anyway, he doubted whether Shechem, injured and muddled as he was, was yet capable of planning a trick.

'Can you find the way out?' he asked.

The answer was hesitant. 'I don't know, without a light.'

Now was the moment. Septimus moved cautiously backwards and stood up.

'I have a light,' he said, and switched on the pencil torch. The beam was blinding in the blackness. It wavered a moment over the rock floor and came to rest on Shechem. He was lying on his side, propped on one elbow, the fingers of his other hand exploring the wound on his head. He scrambled to his feet. 'Then we can get out,' he said. 'Come on, Mr Treloar, before the other one comes back. He's somewhere in the mine. I know he is. I can tell.'

Septimus made no answer to this, but he thought grimly to himself, 'Yes, I know he is. And he might come back any time.'

'Give me the light, Mr Treloar.'

'No,' replied Septimus, hastily casting his answer in an infantile form. 'No. It's my light, and I'm going to keep it.' By putting it that way he avoided mentioning his utter distrust of Shechem's new-found docility.

Shechem accepted the childish answer without comment. 'Come on, then,' he said. 'Shine the light on the floor.' He took a moment to orient himself, and then they moved slowly side by side across the cavern, up the gentle slope and away from the water. They came to a narrow tunnel which was so low that Shechem had to stoop to enter it. Septimus followed, his torch on Shechem's back. Shechem must be moving into almost total blackness, but it did not seem to trouble him. He must know that there was no obstruction in the tunnel. The roof came lower as they went forward until they were on their hands and knees, and then crawling almost at full length so that Septimus could see only the soles of Shechem's boots, the nails gleaming brightly in the light of the torch. Suddenly the boot soles vanished and the torch was shining on dirty brown corduroy. Septimus switched off the torch and lay still. If 'the other one' had returned, he was going to be quite helpless as he crawled out of the hole.

'Come on, Mr Treloar.' Shechem's voice sounded distant,

and it echoed as if he were standing in a big cavern. Septimus produced the mental equivalent of a shrug of the shoulders. There was absolutely nothing he could do to protect himself. He crawled forward and stood up.

Shechem was waiting beside the tunnel mouth leaning against a pile of broken rock.

'The other one and I found that tunnel,' he said proudly. 'I moved the rocks. He helped me.'

'Lead on,' said Septimus abruptly. He wanted to keep Shechem's mind off the 'other one'.

They had come out into a large slate cavern and Shechem led the way across it, Septimus beside him, the pencil beam of the torch glancing across the rock before their feet and up the rough slate walls, blue and shadowed in the meagre light.

'The other one is called Cain,' whispered Shechem. Septimus saw him look back furtively over his shoulder. 'I know why he hit you, Mr Treloar. It was because the tunnel is so narrow, and because he didn't know how to get you across the bridge. Cain is bad, Mr Treloar. And he's about the place somewhere. I know he is.'

Desperately Septimus tried to change the direction of Shechem's thoughts.

'The bridge,' he said. 'Yes. I suppose these chambers lead to the bridge. I expect it used to be much bigger. Did they carry slate over it, Shechem?'

'Oh, yes. My father told me. He used to work down here. Lots of men. Lots of slate. But now it's all empty. Nothing and nobody. Just the rock falls and the water. Only the other one lives here now. And the gods.'

'Shall we soon come to the bridge?'

'Not far now.'

In fact they walked through seven slate chambers, up a short, steep incline and along a tunnel before the slim beam of the torch revealed the chasm and the wreck of the bridge. There was more of it remaining than there had been on the other side. It hung down, a tangle of rusty girders and rotten timber disappearing into the chasm beyond the range of the torch.

'I'll go first and then light you across,' Septimus said. It seemed the least dangerous way round. Shechem made no reply, and Septimus shone the torch on to the baulk of timber and walked swiftly across, looking neither to right nor left. It was easier than he expected. With the torch only lighting the grey surface of the timber, there was little feeling of the yawning chasm in the blackness. It was, even so, a relief to get to the other side and turn and shine the torch for Shechem.

'Come on,' he said. Shechem did not move. 'Listen!' His voice was a hiss, and Septimus could sense terror in the sound. He flicked the beam of the torch on to the other man. He was half crouched, staring into the blackness behind him. 'Listen!' It was so insistent that Septimus found himself trying to isolate some sound in the silence which was the partner of the darkness under the earth.

But — yes. There was a sound. A distant murmur, so faint that you could only hear it because there was no other sound to mask it. Septimus recognized it for what it was.

'It's him! He's talking to himself. He does talk to himself. He's coming, Mr Treloar.'

'Rubbish!' Septimus shouted in his anxiety. 'It's only the waterfall beyond the rock slip.'

'No! No! It's him. It's the other. It's Cain.'

Septimus sounded as calm as a skilled nurse dealing with a fractious child. 'You'd better come over the bridge then. Leave Cain on that side.' Shechem did not move. Septimus sharpened his tone.

'Come on, Shechem. The torch won't last for ever.'

Shechem came on to the bridge at a shambling run, Septimus doing what he could to help with the beam of the torch. Shechem reached the middle and stopped abruptly, his boots skidding on the wood, his body swaying.

'Listen,' he said again, but this time it was almost calm,

and the childish quality had gone out of his voice. 'Listen. He's calling me.' He turned precariously on the narrow beam, swaying over the gulf, totally unaware of his danger. He started to walk back into the darkness.

Septimus bellowed, his voice echoing and rumbling in the caverns.

'Shechem! There's nothing. Come here at once.' Such was his authority that the words penetrated Shechem's clouded mind. He stopped and started to turn back. As he turned, Septimus ran on to the beam, heedless of the danger to himself, reaching out for Shechem's arm.

He was too late.

Shechem thrust out both arms in front of his face as if he would ward off an attack. 'Aah!' he cried. 'Aah!', a great shout echoing from the rock, and even as Septimus grabbed at the outstretched arms, his boots slid from the beam. Septimus saw arms whirling in the light of the torch, then he lost his own balance and fell across the beam, his head and arms on one side, his legs on the other.

As he fell he clenched his fist on the torch, an automatic reaction, the drowning man clutching at a straw, but the light had gone out. There was only blackness, and out of the blackness a terrible, fading scream. Then there was a thump and the scream was cut off, then – a long time after, it seemed – there was a distant splash. Then there was silence.

Septimus lay a moment, trembling with the shock and horror of what had happened. Then with great care he inched his whole body back on to the beam, first his hands and then his legs, and so crawled to the safety of the ravine side. Knowing the futility of it, he shouted and flashed his torch into the chasm. His calls brought no reply, and the torch revealed nothing, no glimmer of water, only the rock walls going down into the darkness. He was alone and She-chem was dead, his broken body floating in the dark waters of the flooded lower levels of the mine.

Septimus rested awhile, sitting by the chasm, his back

against the rock wall. Now that he was safe – if not from the dangers of the mine, at least from Shechem – he was conscious of a sense of failure. He was moved by pity. Shechem might have been crazy, murderously crazy, but at least he had tried to save the things he loved. Yet there was a certain fitness in his death. Had they both escaped from the mine, that would have been the end of Shechem's liberty. It would have had to be so. Yet it would have been a terrible cruelty to immure him in some close-security mental hospital, like a wild thing in an iron cage. It was probably better this way. He prayed a moment, commending Shechem into the hands of God. If mercy and understanding were to be found beyond the mystery of death, he had no manner of doubt that Shechem would find them.

He stood up, putting Shechem from his mind by a firm act of will, concentrating now on trying to remember the details of the journey down from the entrance to the mine. He could recall the route with reasonable clarity, but the blow on the jaw seemed to have driven the figures out of his mind. He rehearsed the route. He was in the original tunnel on Level Six. Because of the rock fall, he had to go down to Level Seven and then up again. The tunnel in which he was standing led to an incline which he must descend. Then he must turn right and pass through three caverns. He must go up an incline, and this should bring him out by the waterfall. Then there was the dangerous tunnel, the one with the rock falls, and that led to – what had Shechem called it? – the adit. Then he should be out. It sounded all right, but there were a lot of places where he could go wrong, and the tiny batteries of his torch would not last for ever. Well . . . he might as well make a start. He switched on the torch and moved slowly away from the chasm.

In the event it was not so difficult as he had expected. Since the mine was designed for the extraction of slate, there was a fairly obvious logic about the tramway lines which all led – eventually – to exits. He realized this when he had struggled precariously down the incline to Level Seven and was confronted by a division in the track, and was not sure which route to follow. With a piece of slate he scratched an arrow on the rusty rail pointing in the direction from which he had come. He set off along what he hoped was the right route, but it ended in a cavern from which there was no exit, a crumbling slate truck half full of rubble standing where the rails ended. He retraced his steps to the point and followed the other line.

It took a long time because he moved cautiously and he was using the torch as little as possible, wanting to conserve the batteries.

He went wrong twice more, and both times the rails he was following disappeared under piles of fallen rock, but at last he came to the waterfall. Then with the light of the torch waning fast he made his way along the dangerous tunnel and turned right into the adit. The going was easier now, for the adit had been cut from the rock of the mountain, as secure and solid as if it had been made from concrete. Now that it did not matter, he remembered that it was eight hundred and three paces to the entrance, but he did not bother to count. The tunnel curved and as he came round the curve he could see far ahead a tiny pinpoint of light. It glowed like a diamond on black velvet. It was the tunnel mouth. As he saw it, so the control that he had exercised for so many hours deserted him. Heedless of all danger, the tears streaming down his face, he broke into a shambling run towards the blessedness of light and away from the black horrors behind him.

So he came at last to the entrance, and leaned out, and heard the wind sighing over the mountainside and the crying of the sheep. The sky to the east was tinged pink with the dawn.

16

Home-coming

'Damn the doctor,' said Septimus, 'I've got to see Dylan, and I'm getting up now. So May Parry, if you don't want to see a clergyman in his underpants you'd better get out.' May Parry's expostulations about what the doctor had said were abruptly cut off as Septimus threw back the bedclothes. She bolted from the room and closed the door behind her. 'Lord save us! What a wilful man!' she said.

Despite the urgency of what he had to do, Septimus dressed slowly. He had to. He was covered with bruises, and he winced with the stiffness of muscles he did not even know he possessed. He looked at himself in the mirror and frowned at what he saw, and winced again because the frown hurt. There was an ugly purple bruise down the side of his face and his right eye was closed.

He had met the search party as he had shambled slowly down into the quarry, a business-like-looking group of men with lamps and tools and wearing miners' helmets. There had been Gwillym Parry, and John and Dylan Wesley Jones, and several others, including Sandy who looked so ridiculous with a lamp on his hat above the white military moustache that Septimus had wanted to giggle. It was at that precise moment that he had realized two facts which stuck out like solid rocks in the muddled sea of his exhaustion. First, he was going to lie about what had happened in the mine. He could not think clearly enough to know why he must do so, he only knew that he must. Second, he was too tired to produce a coherent lie on the spur of the moment. So he pretended to be in even worse physical condition than in fact he was, answering as few questions as possible.

Yes, he had gone into the mine with Shechem. Shechem had wanted to show Gwyn something he had found, and Septimus had taken his place because the child was terrified, and Shechem had refused to let him go until Septimus had promised to go with him. It was some sort of cave that Shechem reckoned to have found. He didn't know what it was like because they hadn't got to it. Shechem had fallen into a chasm, and Septimus had spent the night trying to find the way out.

Sandy had been suspicious, knowing Septimus as well as he did.

'How did you get that blow on the face?' he asked. Septimus was too tired to invent a plausible answer, so he had taken the easy way out and pretended to faint.

Now, despite the dilapidated state of his body, his mind was clear after twelve hours' sleep, and he knew why he had lied and what he must do. In his imagination he could see Shechem's mother in the little cottage high in the lonely valley. The death of her son was going to be grief enough to bear. At least, if Septimus could manage it, Shechem's death was going to appear as an accident. The alternative was too vulgar and crude to be borne – the valleys teeming with reporters and gaping sightseers, newspaper headlines about 'Human Sacrifice in Welsh Valley' and 'Death Drama in Old Mine'. He could imagine Evan Pritchard pontificating on Harlech Television. Evan would love that, but why should he earn money from the death of a good man? No, it was far better to turn it into an accident, and the fewer people who knew about it, the better. The lie must stay as close to the truth as possible, and already the details of the story were forming in his mind. It had to be foolproof, and if it was to be, there was one practical thing that had to be done, and he could not do it alone. He would have taken Sandy into his confidence, but for the wooden leg. Of the other possibilities Dylan was the best. He would understand and sympathize with Shechem's motives, and he of all people would wish to preserve the valleys from a squalid scandal.

Septimus finished dressing and went downstairs and out of the Mill, ignoring Sandy's questioning shout. He met John Wesley Jones in the lane and learned that a full-scale search for Shechem's body had been organized for next day. Septimus was impressed. These Welsh slate miners could move speedily when there was reason. After all, the mine had been closed for years, and in one day they had unearthed and studied the plans, and had collected from the surrounding countryside a group of older men who had worked in it. John Wesley Jones was solicitous about Septimus's injuries. He was blaming himself for the whole disaster. 'I should have kept a closer eye on the child. Indeed I should, and the tragedy is my fault. But that salmon I told you about was rising, and Gwillym and May were not to be back until seven, so I thought there was no harm in it and I landed from the boat, and little Gwyn wandered off, and I was so intent on the salmon that I never missed him.'

So that was the way it had been. As simple as that. Septimus wondered how far Shechem had planned to seize the child — or had it just been a pure chance, which would have seemed to him like the work of the old gods? He would never know now.

'You mustn't blame yourself, John,' he said. 'It might have happened anyway, even if Shechem had gone into the mine alone.'

'Yes. That is true,' said the other man sadly. 'We have a meeting in the Maenofferen Arms to look at the plans and work out what we must do tomorrow.'

'Do you want me to come?' Septimus asked.

'It is not necessary, man. From what you have said it is clear enough where he is. We shall probably go in by the adit on Level Nine – if it has not collapsed, that is.' A sudden smile lit up his grave face. 'And I reckon you have had a bellyful of old slate mines, Mr Treloar.'

'You can say that again,' said Septimus. They parted, Septimus having discovered that Dylan was in the cottage.

Dylan was obviously glad to see him and ushered him courteously into the little parlour.

'I want your help, Dylan,' he said. They sat in front of the fire, and Dylan listened gravely as Septimus told the truth of what had happened, what he wanted to do, and why he wanted to do it. 'It's got to be done tonight,' he concluded, 'before tomorrow's search party. No one must get into that cave because of the ropes and the wood and the smashed lamp. If they do, it'll all come out. And apart from anything else, I shall end up doing time for perjuring myself at the inquest.'

Dylan sat a moment, gazing into the fire, looking uncommonly like his father.

'And it was all unnecessary,' he said sadly.

'What do you mean?'

'I met that surveyor chap in the Maenofferen last night. I apologized to him for being so damn silly. He's quite a nice bloke really. He told me. They'll never build a dam across this valley. There's a fault in the rock big enough to drive a bus through. Wouldn't be safe. But you're quite right about Shechem. It is far better that it should be an accident. Better for the old lady, and for the valleys.'

'We shall need crowbars,' said Septimus, 'and lamps.'

'And safety hats,' said Dylan. 'I can get the equipment without my father knowing about it.'

'We'll go round in Sandy's Land-Rover,' Septimus said, looking at his watch. 'Start at ten o'clock.'

Dylan grinned. 'Man! if we do that, set off in the Colonel's Land-Rover with crowbars and lamps and miners' hats, all the village will be talking about it tomorrow morning. No. We'll go at midnight, and we'll row across in my father's

151

boat. You can tell the Colonel you're going poaching salmon with Gwillym Parry.'

'Poaching salmon?' said Sandy, his voice sharp with incredulity. 'You're a bloody liar, Septimus, what are you up to?'

Septimus agreed amicably. 'Yes, I am a bloody liar, but that's my story and I'm sticking to it. As far as you're concerned, I'm fast asleep in my bed – where all good parsons are at midnight. And you just keep saying that when they put you on the rack.'

'I'll lie for old-times' sake,' replied the soldier, 'but I would like to know why. You didn't tell the truth about what happened in the mine, did you?'

Septimus was serious now. 'No, I didn't. But it matters, Sandy. Like security. I'd tell you as an old friend – of course I would, and of course I can trust you. But you know the principles. Dammit all, man! You taught me them! "Nobody must know, who does not have to know. What you do not know cannot be divulged by accident, or extracted by trickery or torture." '

Sandy smiled. 'Fair enough. Hoist on my own wooden leg, aren't I? Get off to bed, old son. I'll leave the kitchen door in case you walk in your sleep, and I hope it stays fine for you.'

Dylan was waiting for him in the boathouse, the equipment already loaded, the oars ready in the rowlocks, the rowlocks muffled with rags. It was dark and still as they rowed in silence across the lake. There was no wind, and the moon was behind clouds. They grounded the boat on the tiny apron of shingle below the end of the scree path and struggled up the steep slope to the adit entrance.

Septimus had been wondering how he would react to entering the mine again. In the event he found it easy. The fear of the unknown had vanished, he had a companion whom he could trust, and the bright, modern lamps banished the shadows from the tunnels, and with the shadows they banished the fear, except for the rational fear of possible rock falls.

Dylan swore softly in Welsh as they turned from the adit into the first, the dangerous tunnel with its piles of fallen rock and its rusting steel bracing.

'Man! This is dangerous.'

Septimus strode on ahead, saying nothing. He knew it was dangerous, but the quicker they got on with it, the sooner they would be out again into safety.

They went through the tunnels, down and up the inclines, and across the chambers where the shadows of the rock pillars marched away from them into the distance, until at last they stood again by the chasm where Shechem had fallen.

'This is the place,' Septimus said.

Dylan leaned out over the edge, holding his lamp at arm's length, turning the powerful beam downward. It was a beacon, a lighthouse in comparison with Septimus's little pocket torch, but even so its light was lost in the depths below. 'They'll be lucky if they find the water at Level Nine,' he said, 'Level Twelve more like. And I'll be surprised if they find his body. It's a natural fissure, Septimus. You can see — the rock's not cut. Might be hundreds of feet deep.'

'Let's get on with it,' said Septimus. He was eager to be away from the place.

It did not take long. With the crowbars they prised the half-rotten baulk of timber from its slot in the rock and sent it crashing from side to side of the chasm until it splashed into the water far below. Septimus remembered the other splash.

'There,' said Dylan. 'No one will get into that cave now. It can keep its secrets.' Suddenly, surprisingly, he thrust out a hand. 'You are a wise man, Septimus, and a good one. I would like to shake hands with you.'

Septimus took the proffered hand. 'Thanks for your help,' he said.

'Let's go,' said Dylan.

153

Septimus replied a little diffidently. 'There is one other thing before we do go,' he said.

'What's that?'

'I intend to say the burial service.'

If Dylan was surprised, he did not show it. 'A very right and proper idea,' he said.

Septimus took his Office Book from his pocket and started the Anglican service for the Burial of the Dead. The measured cadences of Jacobean English echoed through the tunnels, with only Dylan – and presumably God – to hear them. 'I am the resurrection and the life saith the Lord . . .' Septimus chose the *De Profundis* as the most appropriate of the possible psalms. 'Out of the deep have I called unto thee, O Lord: Lord, hear my voice.' It was a professional task, and for all the strangeness of the situation, he read the service well. Professionalism was in his blood. He only made one change. When he came to the committal, he used not the set form, but the ancient words for a burial at sea. '. . . We therefore commit his body to the deep, earth to earth, ashes to ashes, dust to dust, in sure and certain hope of the resurrection to eternal life . . .' He ended the office and closed the book with a little thump. Dylan, who had stood with his head bowed, and as still as a statue carved from the surrounding rock, looked up with a little grin on his lips.

'Very affecting, Septimus. I have never heard the English service before. But it was in my mind while you were reading it that Shechem – if he was anything – was probably a Welsh Baptist. I do not think he would have approved of a read service, man.'

Septimus knew that the joke was being made as a mask for deeper emotions, and so he changed the subject.

'While I was reading it,' he said, 'something struck me. Look at that.' He pointed the beam of his lantern to the slot in the rock from which they had prised the baulk of timber.

'What about it?'

154

'It's too square. No one with any sense would ever believe that the beam came out of that by accident.'

Dylan stooped, examining the slot. 'By God!' he said softly. 'It may not have fallen out by nature, but it soon would. Look at this!' He was pointing to a crack in the rock which at its widest was a full two inches from side to side. 'The whole edge of the cliff could slide at any time.'

'No time like the present,' Septimus said.

They put the crowbars in the crack and levered with all their strength. The rock groaned and trembled, then with a sharp crack it came free and slid into the abyss, and for the third and last time Septimus heard a splash from the unseen water far below.

He stooped, examining the edge where the crack had been. The marks of the crowbars were plain to see. He rubbed them smooth with a piece of slate and then smeared the scratch marks with a piece of rotten wood. Certainly it would not fool a suspicious detective, but it was adequate for any cursory examination that was likely to be made.

Septimus took one last look across the chasm, thinking of the darkness of the cave of the Stone of Offering. As Dylan said, it could keep its secrets now. If in the future men entered it again, Shechem would be forgotten and they would make nothing of what they found there.

'Come on,' said Dylan. 'Let's get out of here.'

Obediently Septimus followed him.

The inquest was held in a strangely tidy bar-parlour of the Maenofferen Arms. The Coroner was a Welsh lawyer from Dolgellau, a percipient man with a shining bald head and a face like a ferret. Septimus was at his most bland and most precise. He had even managed to borrow a clerical collar from a minister in Blaenau Ffestiniog, after some difficulty in finding a Welsh clergyman with a large enough neck. He told his fellow cleric that he thought he ought to be properly dressed for such a solemn occasion as an inquest. What he really had in mind was that the dog-collar would add an air of authenticity to the lies he was proposing to tell.

There was only one awkward moment at the inquest when the Coroner got on to the question of why Septimus had gone into the mine with Shechem.

'But you knew it was very dangerous, Mr Treloar.'

'Yes, sir.'

'Then why did you go? Into a dangerous mine? With a man you knew to be mentally unstable?'

'Because he insisted that I accompany him.'

'Insisted?'

Innocent blue eyes gazed at the Coroner over the white-washed stockade of the borrowed clerical collar. 'He said he'd thump me if I didn't.' The dangerous moment passed in a titter of laughter, which the Coroner brought to an end out of respect for Shechem's mother who was in the court.

John Wesley Jones gave evidence about the search for Shechem's body. They had had no success. All the adits below Level Six were either collapsed, flooded, or far too dangerous to enter. Yes, they had gone in on Level Six and examined the top of the chasm. Yes, they had seen where the beam had fallen from the rock. It was just as Mr Treloar had said it was. There followed a series of questions which served to demonstrate how little the Coroner knew about slate mines. Septimus could see that John Wesley Jones was beginning to get irritated.

'You could not get down this chasm as you call it?'

'No, sir, not being spiders.' That brought a laugh. The Coroner frowned round the bar-parlour.

'Could it not be descended with the proper equipment? With ladders and scaffolding?'

John Wesley Jones' control broke.

'Man! if you give a gang of Welsh miners the right equipment and time enough, they'll climb down into Hell for you! But what I want to know is – who's going to pay for it all?'

The verdict was 'Death by misadventure', and the Coroner added some of the customary Coroner's remarks, banality vying with futility for pride of place, in this case about the dangers of casual persons entering disused mines.

Outside the court Septimus was arguing with Sandy, explaining why he must return home on the following day. 'I've got Sunday services to take, Sandy. Can't expect the neighbours to do my work for ever.' Out of the corner of his eye he saw Shechem's mother. He broke off his conversation with Sandy and went to her. She was dressed as she had been when he last saw her, except that she was wearing a black veil, which made her look even more like Queen Victoria. She showed no more emotion than she had done before.

'I am sorry,' he said.

'And why should you be sorry, Mr Treloar?'

'I would have saved his life if I could.'

She did not answer for a moment, and when she did, he could see beneath the veil that there was a ghost of a smile on her lips. 'Then thank you for saving his name. I did not think to hear such lies from the lips of a minister of religion, and him under oath in a court of law.'

'It depends what you mean by lies, mother,' said Septimus gravely, 'but I see that you know.'

'Know? I know nothing except that Shechem is dead. I can guess, but guessing is without point.'

'Do you wish to know? I will tell you if you wish it, mother.' He spoke humbly, aware of his utter ignorance.

'No. It is better as it is. An accident under the mountain. Whatever he did, Shechem intended good.'

'That is true,' Septimus replied.

'Then thank you for what you did – and for what you tried to do.'

Septimus did not reply because he could think of nothing to say.

She turned away and went to the ridiculous old bicycle

157

propped against the wall. Septimus watched her mount and ride slowly out of the village.

It was early evening when he arrived home after the long drive across Wales and England. He drove his own Land-Rover round the well-remembered potholes of Danedyke St Mary's Rectory drive, and switched off the engine outside his own front door. The rooks were coming home to the elms between the Rectory and the church, and he could hear the sound of a tractor in the distance. Harry Garner on the Home Farm was working late on his spring ploughing.

The front door opened and Rosemary Barton came out. She was looking prettier than ever, and his absence from home had given time for him to confirm his suspicions. Rosemary was going to have a baby. And a jolly good job too. Her glad greeting broke off in astonishment.

'Rector! Look at your face . . .' Septimus parried the coming question.

'Hullo, Rosemary. I can't look at my face without a mirror.'

Rosemary scolded him. 'Septimus! You've been fighting.' She made it sound as if he had been doing it in the playground.

'Fell down a Welsh hillside,' he said simply.

'Did you have a good rest?'

Grace, his half-grown Great Dane saved him from answering that one. She came through the door like a fighting bull into an arena, and hurled herself incontinently at his chest, nearly knocking him headlong. She put her paws on his shoulders and licked his face. 'Get down, you stupid old fool,' he growled.

They went into the Rectory.

Rosemary had cooked him a macaroni cheese, knowing it was his favourite dish. She brought it into the dining-room at the run, because of the heat of the dish. 'Don't burn yourself, Septimus.'

'Well, Rosemary, what's happened while I've been away?'

'Little Johnny Thomas has got scarlet fever of all things. And — Septimus — the magazine's due next Tuesday.'

He helped himself to macaroni cheese. It was good to be home.